A Home Subscription! It's the easiest and most convenient way to get every one of the exciting Coventry Romance Novels! ...And you get 4 of them FREE!

You pay nothing extra for this convenience; there are no additional charges...you don't even pay for postage! Fill out and send us the handy coupon now, and we'll send you 4 exciting Coventry Romance novels absolutely FREE!

SEND NO MONEY, GET THESE
FOUR BOOKS
FREE!

━━ ━━ ━━ ━━ ━━ ━━ ━━ ━━ ━━ ━━ ━━ ━━ ━━ ━━ ━━

C1080

**MAIL THIS COUPON TODAY TO:
COVENTRY HOME
SUBSCRIPTION SERVICE
6 COMMERCIAL STREET
HICKSVILLE, NEW YORK 11801**

YES, please start a Coventry Romance Home Subscription in my name, and send me FREE and without obligation to buy, my 4 Coventry Romances. If you do not hear from me after I have examined my 4 FREE books. please send me the 6 new Coventry Romances each month as soon as they come off the presses. I understand that I will be billed only $10.50 for all 6 books There are no shipping and handling nor any other hidden charges. There is no minimum number of monthly purchases that I have to make In fact. I can cancel my subscription at any time. The first 4 FREE books are mine to keep as a gift. even if I do not buy any additional books.

For added convenience. your monthly subscription may be charged automati cally to your credit card.

☐ Master Charge   ☐ Visa

Credit Card # _____

Expiration Date _____

Name _____
(Please Print)

Address _____

City _____ State _____ Zip _____

Signature _____

☐ Bill Me Direct Each Month

This offer expires March 31. 1981 Prices subject to change without notice Publisher reserves the right to substitute alternate FREE books. Sales tax col lected where required by law. Offer valid for new members only.

DEBT OF LOVE

Rachelle Edwards

FAWCETT COVENTRY • NEW YORK

DEBT OF LOVE

Published by Fawcett Coventry Books, a unit of CBS Publications, the Consumer Publishing Division of CBS Inc., by arrangement with Robert Hale Limited

ISBN: 0-449-50108-6

Printed in the United States of America

First Fawcett Coventry printing: October 1980

15 14 13 12 11 10 9 8 7 6 5 4 3 2 1

One

Lady Clyde did not really expect to find Sir Francis Derringham at home when she called at his house in Albermarle Street, so it was with great pleasure that she greeted him as she was ushered into the spacious library. Under one arm she held a small dog which went with her everywhere.

Six Francis Derringham was a handsome man of some thirty-eight years, much despaired of by husband-seeking debutantes and youthful widows, for his imposing appearance was over-shadowed only by his wealth and prominent status in London Society.

On this particular morning, freshly-shaven by his valet, he wore a plain buff-coloured coat which was very much the new vogue, and a silk ribbon to hold back his own hair.

Lady Clyde beamed as he rose from his seat at the desk where he had been perusing frowningly a sheet of parchment. As the footman closed the door behind her, she cried, "Francis, my dear! What a pleasant surprise, for I was quite resolved to leave a card for you."

The little dog growled, causing Sir Francis to draw back. "Oh, do be quiet, Didi," the marchioness scolded.

Sir Francis waved his hand in the air. "As usual he will not allow me close to you."

"Didi is very fond of you, only he is a mite jealous of anyone who comes near to me."

One of the baronet's eyebrows went up a fraction. "I would appreciate that sentiment more in a husband. Now, my dear, to what do I owe this honour?"

The marchioness handed the dog to the page who accompanied her. "Take Didi outside, Oswald. I fear he and Sir Francis will never be friends."

Sir Francis watched them go with some relief and then once again gave his attention to Lady Clyde. "I simply had to say how everyone enjoyed our theatrical soiree last night. You made a splendid Sir Peter Teazle!"

He smiled faintly as he came to greet her at last, taking her hand and pressing it to his lips. "It is kind of you to say so, my dear, but I doubt if Tom King need fear for his reputation."

She laughed. "You, at least, do not have to suffer catcalls from the pit." She looked at him curiously then. "I had thought you would be about your business at this hour."

"So I am," he answered, looking down at her in some amusement.

She turned back towards the door. "Say no more! I shall be on my way immediately to buy a new hat."

"I am certain it will become you, but you need no gilding, Virginia."

"Flatterer." She looked nonetheless pleased.

He moved away from her then. "In fact I am glad you came. You are the one person with whom I would talk today."

She frowned although this scarcely marred her looks. Gowned in blue velvet with a matching feathered bonnet atop her powdered curls, she was acknowledged a Beauty even amongst those whose tastes were particularly discerning.

"I thought I detected an odd mood in you. Is something amiss?"

In answer he moved two chairs closer to the fire before ushering her to one of them. As she continued to look at him curiously he went to stand by the mantel. He turned slightly to look into the fire so that his face was in profile.

"Do you recall someone by the name of Colonel Hubert Wentworth?"

Lady Clyde frowned. "Wentworth? The name is exceeding familiar. Wentworth . . .?"

"He married a lady by the name of Katherine Avebury—oh some twenty years ago."

She let out a long sigh and then smiled. "Of course I recall. She was, if I remember rightly, very beautiful. How I envied her! He was possessed of a modest fortune, but if my memory does not serve me wrong I recall he was an odd fellow and not at all suited to a high-flyer like Miss Avebury."

"He was not easy to know."

"I wonder what happened to them."

"They decided on a life of rustication on Colonel Wentworth's Devonshire estate."

Lady Clyde became alert. "Oh, do tell me! Colonel Wentworth and his wife are come back to London. Is that it?"

Sir Francis brought out his jewelled snuff box and took a pinch before answering. "Colonel Wentworth is recently deceased."

Her face fell. "Oh, I am sorry to hear you say so. And his wife?"

"Dead years ago."

"Oh, so this is the news which has afflicted you so sorely. I recall well now how much in love you were with Mrs. Wentworth."

Sir Francis moved away from the mantel now. "I was no more than a giddy youth, Virginia, in love with many."

Lady Clyde looked disbelieving. "Francis! I remember one night when you actually slept on her doorstep, just so you could be the first admitted to her toilette the following morning. And you made a great cake of yourself for ever dogging her footsteps wherever she went."

He smiled then. "I cannot conceive that I was such a fool."

"You were not alone in your foolishness, but there were times when Mama and I thought you were fit only for Bedlam. Even now there are those who cannot believe you are, by comparison, a sober-minded person!" She frowned suddenly. "I wonder why they left London. Do you know anything about it?"

"No," he answered thoughtfully, "but you might think me foolish if I venture to say Colonel Wentworth was jealous of his wife's success."

"La! If every married man looked upon his wife in such a manner the Season would crumble."

He continued to look thoughtful. "It is only a notion which occurred to me. It might well bear no reality to the truth."

Lady Clyde looked at him with concern as he walked slowly to the desk. "It is sad to hear of their demise, Francis, but it is a very long time since we saw either of them."

He picked up the parchment he had been

studying when she arrived, stared at it for a moment or two before looking at Lady Clyde once again.

"A letter arrived this morning—from a lawyer in Exeter . . ."

"Regarding the Wentworths?"

"Yes," he answered heavily. "It would seem they had a child—Robin. His guardianship has been awarded to me."

Lady Clyde stared at him uncomprehendingly for a moment or two before she threw back her head and laughed heartily. The sound of her laughter filled the room, echoing around the marble columns and book-filled cabinets. Sir Francis snatched up the letter from the desk and strode across the room.

"I had hoped to have counsel with you, Virginia, not merriment. It is an exceeding serious matter."

Her laughter died but she still smiled. She touched his hand as he sat down at last by her side. "Forgive me, dearest. It was merely the thought of *you*—who must have been the wildest rake in London when Colonel Wentworth knew you—being given guardianship of his child."

"I know. It is the oddest occurrence. I am at a loss what to do."

Her eyes narrowed. "Why you, Francis? Apart from your fleeting passion for Mrs. Wentworth I can conceive of no reason why you should be selected. You were hardly acquainted with Colonel Wentworth."

He shook his head. "The lawyer states in his letter that Colonel Wentworth deemed me the 'person best qualified to be his child's guardian'. Best qualified indeed! The fellow's attic must have been to let when he worded his will. What am I to do, Virginia? I am neither fitted nor willing to be guardian to a young boy."

Lady Clyde gave him an amused look. "No doubt Colonel Wentworth imagined you wedded by now with a brood of your own."

"But I am not and I have not the slightest notion what I must do."

"There must be relatives who would be willing to care for the boy. As his legal guardian you could merely retain a token say in his affairs."

"The lawyer indicates that there are no relatives left alive who are fitted to the task. That is why Colonel Wentworth was obliged to seek outside the family circle for a guardian."

She waved her hand vaguely in the air. "I really cannot understand why you are in such a pucker over this; it is like you will only have to travel to Devonshire once or twice a year to oversee his progress."

"Virginia," he said with great patience, "Robin Wentworth has already embarked upon his journey to London."

Her hand flew to her lips. "Oh, my dear, I am

so sorry. I had no notion that matters were so far advanced." She took the letter from him and perused it carefully. "This tells you precious little about the boy or his situation, save that his fortune is respectable, but twenty-five is a little old for him to come into it."

"Wentworth always appeared to be a careful soul."

"Have you consulted your lawyer as yet?"

"Farthingale left here not ten minutes before you arrived. Of course, no one can *make* me accept responsibility for the bra . . . boy . . ."

Lady Clyde hesitated before saying, "It is all too bad, but you do know there is little you can do about it now. You are honour bound."

He nodded. "Yes, indeed, that is precisely it, but it remains that I know nothing about small boys."

"Oh, come now," she said rallyingly, "you have always dealt quite handsomely with my own dear Charles."

He smiled slightly again. "Only recollect, Virginia, your son is almost a man and he is so rarely at home."

"So it will be with Master Wentworth. You will not be required to be his nursemaid, Francis. No doubt he will be travelling with his tutor who will be his immediate companion. I am quite convinced you will make arrangements for him to go to Eton as soon as you are able."

She shrugged slightly. "Cambridge or Oxford will follow that and then a Grand Tour. By the time he returns to London he will be ready to take his place in Society, and you will be glad to know him at last. For the moment you need not know he is here!"

Sir Francis took up her hand and raised it to his lips. "My dear, I knew I could rely on your counsel. You are a genius."

She laughed delightedly before saying, "Now, if your nursery was filled you would not have this vexing problem."

"No, by jove! I would have a hundred more!"

She laughed again and then caught sight of the ormolu mantel clock. With her silk skirts rustling beneath her velvet gown she hastily got to her feet.

"I must hurry now for I am late for an appointment with my milliner."

He walked with her to the door. "I am obliged to you for your time and your advice, my dear."

"Tush! There is always time for you, my favourite cousin, although it would be far better if you had a wife to give you counsel."

"A wife, I am persuaded, would give me nothing but heartache."

"It is as well other men do not think as you do, or there would be little future to look forward to."

"It is merely that I have never found sufficient reason to become leg-shackled."

"The Derringham jewels are several good reasons, locked away for the want of someone to wear them. 'Tis a shameful waste."

"There is only one perfect spouse and she is married to Lord Clyde. All others pale beside her."

"Faddle!" she responded delightedly. "You must think about the future—your need for an heir if nothing else—before it is too late."

"Remind me again in about forty years time. It will just be the right time, I fancy."

She smiled wryly. "You are impossible."

"And you, I am persuaded, dear Virginia, would not take kindly to being ousted as the most important woman in the life of Sir Francis Derringham."

Her eyebrows arched in surprise. "Your taking of a wife would not alter that, Francis." Her face wrinkled into a smile. "Do not forget to have the nursery and the schoolroom prepared in good time, and do let me know when the boy arrives. Recall he may feel lost at the recent events in his life."

"No more than I," Sir Francis responded.

As she went out of the library and took possession of her dog once more she looked at him mockingly. "You should be thankful, my dear; Colonel Wentworth might have had a daughter!"

*   *   *

14

Several days after his conversation with Lady Clyde, Sir Francis arrived home to find the house in something of a turmoil. As he surveyed the calling cards which had been left in his absence he became aware of a great hurry-scurry all around him. At first he merely thought it must be the usual hurry to light the hundreds of candles at the approach of nightfall, for footmen and maids ran to and fro in great excitement. Sir Francis let the cards drop from his fingers, realising suddenly that the moment he had dreaded for days must have arrived.

He glanced at the head footman who had received his hat, gloves and cane and detected a hint of a smile on the man's face.

"Do you find something amusing, Fosgill?"

The man's face immediately became an inscrutible mask. "No, sir. Nothing, sir."

Sir Francis moved away so he should not be tempted to vent his spleen on the unfortunate lackey. As he crossed the hall his housekeeper came hurrying down the stairs, her keys clanking at her belt.

"Sir Francis," she said breathlessly, sinking into a curtsey.

The baronet paused to take a pinch of snuff before saying, "Ah yes, I know, Mrs Maggs, my ward has arrived."

The woman's eyes flashed. "Indeed, sir, and I would beg your presence in the nursery."

"There appears to be no necessity for that, Mrs Maggs; I perceive enough servants attendant on the nursery without my unnecessary presence. I think I shall allow Master Wentworth to settle in a piece before I acquaint myself with him."

"Master Wentworth indeed! Sir Francis, I think you'd best be going now, sir, beggin' your pardon, or there's like to be no nursery left."

He looked at the woman curiously before brushing past her, taking the stairs two at a time. When he reached the second landing two maidservants were hurrying towards him, giggling and laughing between themselves, but when they caught sight of their master they stopped abruptly and made deep curtseys.

As they hurried away, resuming their excited chatter he watched them curiously for a moment or two. For the first time an unwelcome thought came into his head. He had quite naturally assumed that this son of a gentleman would behave in a manner that would enable him to forget the child's existence for most of the time, but now he recalled his own childhood. He had been what his father often described as *enfant terrible*, plaguing the servants with his pranks and generally resisting discipline. If this child was of a similar ilk ... Perspiration broke out on his brow at the very thought that his well-organised life might be shattered by this unwanted burden, and anger flamed inside him. What could Colonel Wentworth have had in his mind?

As he approached the nursery suite he heard a high-pitched voice cry, "This insult is not to be borne! I will not be consigned to the schoolroom."

"My dear," came a soothing voice, "there has obviously been some error, so you must not be in such a taking."

Sir Francis marched purposefully into the suite to be met by a scene of great chaos. Trunks and bandboxes were piled upon the floor, some of which were half-opened, their contents spilling out. A maidservant stood fearfully in a corner and a woman of middle-age, dumpy and gowned in a black bombazine was nearby. In the centre of the room a girl, clad similarly in an ill-fitting gown of black silk, stood, arms akimbo, glaring around her. Her dark eyes were ablaze with anger and her unpowdered curls hung like corkscrews past her waist. She wore no powder, patches or paint on her cheeks, but their colour was high nevertheless.

Sir Francis stood in the doorway, surveying the scene with amazement until the girl caught sight of him and her eyes flashed with anger.

"How many lackeys do I have to address before Sir Francis is summoned? Fetch him now, you fool, or it'll be the worse for you, I vow.

I shall not tolerate this insult a moment longer!"

When he merely stared, the girl stooped down, snatched up a shoe from one of the open trunks and hurled it at him. Sir Francis snapped out of his surprise and immediately ducked, the shoe thudding harmlessly into the wall.

"Oh!" cried the older women, drawing back in alarm. "You should not have done that."

"May I ask what is going on here?" Sir Francis enquired, regaining some of his customary aplomb.

"No, you may not. I am heartily sick of a succession of lackeys. I want to see Sir Francis Derringham now. *Now,* do you understand!"

He made a bow. "At your service, ma'am." He picked up the shoe from where it had fallen. "Even a lackey is not to be greeted in this manner," he told her, becoming momentarily severe. "To be plain, madam, I do not like it."

The older woman gasped. "Oh, Sir Francis, I do beg your pardon most humbly."

It was the girl's turn to be taken aback now. Her eyes grew wide and her cheeks pale. Sir Francis feared she might swoon but it appeared she was made of sterner stuff. He was not so certain about the other woman though. She held up her vinaigrette and swayed uncertainly on her feet.

Moments later the girl rallied. "You cannot be he. Sir Francis was acquainted with Colonel

18

Wentworth and must needs be a much older man."

He bowed again. "You honour me, ma'am, but I am indeed he. Now pray tell me where is my ward—Master Robin Wentworth?"

The girl's face grew red and her eyes bright. "Master Wentworth! *I* am Robyn Wentworth and at seventeen years old I have no intention of being consigned to the schoolroom!"

Although shocked to the very core of his being Sir Francis steeled himself to receive the partner of the shoe he still held.

"*Miss* Wentworth. I was given to understand my ward was a boy."

"R-o-b-y-n," the girl spelled out through clenched teeth. "That lawyer's a senile old fool, and I have oft told him so."

Sir Francis did not doubt it, but his mind was in a whirl. A giggle from the maidservant caused him to turn on his heel.

"You may go," he said severely, and the girl scurried out of the room, stifling her laughter with her hand.

Still numbed by this blow Sir Francis said with a sigh, "Well, we have clarified one matter." He turned to the older woman and bowed stiffly. "Your servant, ma'am."

The woman smile hesitantly but before she could speak Robyn Wentworth said, almost absently, for it appeared she had suffered something of a shock too, "This is my kinswoman, Mrs Fordingbridge."

"I do regret . . ."

"It is of no moment I assure you. I shall see that rooms are prepared for you on the main floor of the house. In the meantime, I would be obliged if you, Miss Wentworth, would desist throwing objects at my servants." He took out his time-piece and glanced at it. "I am engaged for dinner tonight but I would be obliged it you would both join me for a glass of ratafia in the library in an hour's time."

So saying he turned on his heel, his head still reeling from this new blow. He knew he would be obliged to think again very carefully on his plans for his ward.

As he left the nursery suite Robyn Wentworth strode to the door and slammed it shut.

"Oh, my dear," Mrs Fordingbridge began, "your behaviour was quite shocking. What must Sir Francis be thinking of us now?"

"I don't care!"

"You must! We are entirely in his hands now."

The girl wrung her hands together in anguish. "I know that all too well."

"Now we are in London you will be obliged to moderate your manners."

"I shall do no such thing you can be sure," the girl warned her darkly, slamming shut one of the trunks with her foot.

20

"I cannot understand why you have taken such a dislike to Sir Francis—and unseen too! I know the loss of your dear father and the upheaval in your life is a great trial to you, but now you have actually met your guardian you must see he is an utterly charming man and still so young too. I own that it was a pleasant surprise."

Robyn's hands clenched into fists. "Oh, he is everything you say, Aunt Lizzie. Charming, witty and handsome too. It is only what I expected him to be. Do not forget he is a hero too, saving our good King's life. I have oft heard the story, singing his praises. His name will go down in history as the saviour of the King, but he is also an unprincipled rake, gamester and tippler." In a deceptively mild tone of voice she added, "I loathe and despise the man."

Mrs Fordingbridge gasped. "I cannot conceive why, Robyn."

The girl stared darkly into the corner. "Be satisfied that I do and am not like to change my mind."

Accustomed to Robyn's dramatic talents, Mrs Fordingbridge said, "Faddle. You will be of another mind before long. Come, we shall prepare to move to more conducive apartments. As I told you, it was all a dreadful mistake. I, for one, shall enjoy living here, recalling my youth. I feel that Sir Francis will be very condescending towards us."

As she spoke she bustled around the room, oblivious to the fact that Robyn still stared ferociously into the corner. The girl was aware that she was alone in the world with the exquisite knowledge of the truth about Sir Francis Derringham. Despite her hatred of him it was a heady feeling.

Two

Mrs Fordingbridge came hesitantly into the library and looked a mite intimidated by Sir Francis who rose to his feet when she entered. She bobbed a curtsey as he looked expectantly beyond her.

"I note you are alone, Mrs Fordingbridge."

"Robyn begs to be excused, Sir Francis. She travels badly and is quite done-up after our journey. She has the headache and I have given her a small dose of laudanum to soothe it. She was almost asleep when I left her." She smiled hesitantly before adding, "I considered it unwise to disturb her."

Sir Francis listened sympathetically and although he did not believe a word of what the woman had said, murmured, "Although I am sorry to hear of Miss Wentworth's indisposition perhaps it is as well that she is absent on this occasion, for we are now able to discuss various matters with more thoroughness than her presence would allow us to do."

His ward, he knew full well, had deliberately declined to accept his invitation. From the moment he had first clapped eyes on her he had known she was going to be difficult. Had she been a boy he would have known instinctively how to suppress a rebellious nature, but he was at a total loss how to deal severely with a girl of seventeen.

Despite his disturbing thoughts he ushered Mrs Fordingbridge to a comfortable chair. "One must hope she will be recovered by the morrow."

"Oh, I am certain she will."

"And the rooms? I trust you are satisfactorily settled now."

"Indeed, Sir Francis," she enthused. "We are much obliged for your kindness."

"A glass of ratafia, Mrs Fordingbridge?"

The woman drew a sigh. "I thank you, Sir Francis."

When they were both comfortably settled the baronet regarded his glass and mused, "As you know, Mrs Fordingbridge, the arrival of your niece has afforded me something of a shock."

"I understand that, Sir Francis, and to be frank she would have been much better born a boy. Incidentally, I must explain that Robyn is not strictly speaking my niece. Her late father was a distant relative who was kind enough to offer me a home when my own dear husband expired. Naturally, with a young child and no wife it was an arrangement beneficial to us both."

Sir Francis hesitated before asking, "So . . . Mrs Wentworth has been dead for some time."

"Oh, when Robyn was a very small child."

She gulped back the ratafia so quickly Sir Francis felt obliged to refill the glass. As he did so he said, "Forgive me for mentioning this, Mrs Fordingbridge, but is Miss Wentworth's behaviour normally so . . . volatile?"

The woman's cheeks grew red although that could have been caused by the ratafia or the heat of the fire.

"She is not a bad girl, Sir Francis."

He gazed at her sombrely. "I did not say that she was, but such hoydenish manners will not do here in London."

"I have already informed her of it, but she has always been a headstrong chit. Colonel Wentworth took no interest in her whatsoever, and she had no Mamma to counsel her. I, regretfully, could never control her as I should."

"Did she not have a governess?"

"Only until she was old enough to go to an academy. Colonel Wentworth was most insistent that she be educated away from home. It was almost as if he did not want her there although we never spoke of the matter. Unfortunately at first Robyn disliked boarding quite heartily and she was rather badly behaved. Colonel Wentworth was obliged to send her to several establishments before she settled, and I am bound to say during the past two years she has been a model pupil."

Mrs Fordingbridge sighed. "She was recalled only when it became apparent that her father would soon expire. Poor child. She was sorely afflicted, which I own surprised me. They were never close, but after she had spoken with him for the last time 'twas obvious she was much moved. She would not come out of her room for three whole days and refused even to attend the funeral."

A silence hung in the air for a moment or two before Sir Francis asked in a thoughtful tone, "Mrs Fordingbridge, do you have any notion why Colonel Wentworth chose me as his daughter's guardian?"

The woman seemed surprised at such a question. "I assume it was because you and he were acquainted in the past."

"Barely."

She looked surprised again before smiling foolishly. "Perchance he considered you best placed to launch her into Society."

Sir Francis put down his glass and on seeing

Mrs Fordingbridge had once again emptied hers, proceeded to fill it, something at which she did not protest.

"As you see, this is a bachelor establishment."

"Yes, indeed, but Colonel Wentworth would not have known."

"It is only a pity he did not take it upon himself to find out."

The woman hesitated before venturing, "I must confess, Sir Francis, Colonel Wentworth in his later years was not . . . how shall I say . . . ?"

Sir Francis looked interested. *"Compos mentis?"* he supplied eagerly.

"A little vague," she amended. "He was given to being confused and occasionally did odd things."

Sir Francis frowned before saying, "If that is the case then it is possible the terms of his will can be broken."

She was startled now and looked up from her enjoyment of the ratafia. "Oh no, Sir Francis. No. Colonel Wentworth was not insane, and I doubt if you could find evidence to suggest it. It was very rash of me to say what I did. He spoke of you frequently and in glowing terms too, enumerating all your splendid qualities."

The baronet sighed as the hope died. He stroked his chin thoughtfully. It had been a very faint hope in any event.

Moments later she went on, quickly now, apparently made bold by the effects of the liqueur. "I appreciate this burden was not looked for by you, Sir Francis, but I do beseech you not to seek a way out of it, for Robyn has no kin apart from myself and she badly needs the guidance I am unable to give her."

He was already fully aware of this but that did not prevent Mrs Fordingbridge's words causing him a great deal of discomfort.

"Robyn has always been prey to hoydenish ways, but I trust that will soon be remedied by the correct company. You see, she also has the tendency to fall into undesirable company. At Ropesby—her home, you know—she was often to be found in the company of serving wenches —gypsies on one occasion. They were soon driven from the neighbourhood, you may be certain. Perchance her father was sensible of the need for a more genteel life when he entrusted her to your care."

Sir Francis drew a deep sigh and thrust out his booted feet towards the fire. "Have no fear, Mrs Fordingbridge, I shall fulfill my obligations to the girl to the full during the period of my guardianship. She does not seem ill-looking, so it is like she will marry before long and I shall be able to relinquish responsibility for her to a husband."

The thought was a comforting one as it was,

it seemed, to Mrs Fordingbridge for she beamed. "You are so good, Sir Francis. Robyn is the luckiest creature alive."

He smiled wryly. "It does not appear that Miss Wentworth thinks so."

She waved her hand in the air. " 'Tis merely shock and grief which causes her to behave so rashly. You will find her much changed in less than a sen'night, once she appreciates all that London and your patronage has to offer."

Sir Francis privately had his doubts but forbore to say so. "Firstly we must ensure she is fit to be presented to Society, Mrs Fordingbridge. Is her entire wardrobe . . . er . . . similar to the gown she was wearing today?"

The woman's cheeks flushed. "Mourning, you know. It was hurriedly altered from one of her Mama's old gowns. We had no time to do anything other."

"Evidently."

"Robyn was of no assistance; she refused at first even to wear mourning. She has a most unfeminine scorn of what is seemly or indeed fashionable. Many's the time I have pleaded with her to look at fashion plates and choose something modish, but she would not."

"Could not her personal maidservant have influenced her a little?"

Mrs Fordingbridge laughed rather too loudly for elegance. "Robyn has no personal maid, Sir

Francis. She has always cared—if one can use the word—for herself."

"I will have my housekeeper appoint one for her, and I trust you will impress upon her the necessity of retaining a maid. Needless to add, I do not allow my servants to be ill-treated. A scolding is all that is necessary when they transgress."

The woman's face grew red again. "That incident with the shoe was most regrettable, Sir Francis. I shall make quite certain it does not happen again, although in mitigation I must say that you were unfortunate in having seen Robyn at her very worst."

The clock struck the hour and Sir Francis got to his feet. "Perchance we shall need to talk again, ma'am, but for now . . ."

"You have been too kind," she beamed as she got rather unsteadily to her feet.

He walked with her to the door, hiding well his heavy heart. "I am rarely at home for dinner, but feel free to order what you wish. The house is your home—for now. Before long I anticipate the arrival of so many invitations you will scarce have time to lay your head here."

Her eyes glittered with tears. "If only I am able to see that child safely wed, then I shall be truly happy."

"I am certain that time is not too far away."

She looked away. "There is just one thing, Sir

Francis; although I appreciate Robyn must be introduced into the correct circles, I do not think I am the one to achieve it. It is so many years . . ."

He smiled slightly as he opened the door and beckoned to a footman who immediately brought over a branch of candles.

"The fact has already occurred to me, ma'am. There is a lady—a cousin of mine—who may be willing to take up Miss Wentworth. If that is so she will have entry to the highest circles."

Mrs Fordingbridge's eyes glittered with tears once again. "She really does need someone like you to take care of her, Sir Francis. Until a husband can be found, a father figure is sadly lacking in her life."

Sir Francis bit back the angry retort that he had no intention of being any such thing, that he frequently entered into liaisons with girls no older than Robyn Wentworth, but at the adoring look on the woman's face he merely nodded frigidly.

When he had closed the library door behind her he stared into space for a moment or two, realising he could not rely on Mrs Fordingbridge to keep his ward out of his, so far, well-regulated life. He hurried to his desk and, taking up quill and parchment, began to write a frantic note to Lady Clyde.

* * *

"I came as soon as I was able," she told him, "only dear Georgiana called in and was anxious to regale me with all her news! By the by she enjoyed out theatricals so much and hopes we shall have a similar evening before long. Then, of all things, little Didi was sick all over the carpet in my boudoir."

"I do trust it is not serious," Sir Francis said with heavy irony which caused Lady Clyde to look at him askance.

"Silly Oswald had been feeding him marchpane. I was quite desolate to leave him, I must own."

"Oh, I am certain Oswald will survive bearing Didi company."

"Really, Francis, I do not like your sarcasm. It does not become you. Oh, by the by, have you heard about dear Fenella Dodington?"

"No," he answered with great emphasis.

"Well, it does transpire that she was not visiting Paris after all. She and Harry . . ."

Sir Francis, ushering her to a sofa in the small drawing room, had listened patiently enough and was then forced to say, "Dearest prattle-box, will you please listen to *me* now?"

Her face took on a look of injured innocence. "You have never called me *that* before."

"I love to listen to your prattling, but not today. I am in the devil of a fix."

"Fudge!" she answered uncompromisingly. "I

know what it is; your ward is arrived. Really, you men are quite amazing. That one small boy should put you in such a pucker is outside of enough. I fail to believe he could be any more of a monster than you were. When I recall the snails you once put into my bed, and the stones in my shoes . . ."

"Listen to me, Virginia," he hissed and she looked at him in astonishment. "My ward is a female and she is seventeen years old."

Lady Clyde's face took on a look of astonishment and disbelief. "You are gammoning me now, Francis."

He straightened up, reaching for his snuff box. As he took a pinch Lady Clyde's smile faded. "You do not fun, do you?" When he made no reply she said, "This is famous!"

"It is a catastrophe."

She looked at him sharply. "She is here?"

"Oh yes, indeed."

"I trust then that she is suitably chaperoned."

"She is accompanied by a relative, a respectable creature if ineffectual."

Lady Clyde reached for her own diamond-studded snuff box and took a pinch before accepting the glass of ratafia poured for her by her cousin. "What to do now?"

He sat down on the sofa facing her, smoothing down his breeches as he did so. "That is precisely the question I have been asking myself for twenty-four hours. I must, of course, solicit your help."

"Anything, Francis. You know I will do anything to help you."

He smiled and put his hand over hers. "That is something of which I am in dire need."

"Firstly you must tell me what she is like."

He smiled faintly and leaned back against the cushions. "She is much worse than I could have envisaged."

"A rustic; I can well imagine."

"A mere rustic would be no problem. She is unkempt, badly dressed and what is more, Virginia, she has the temper of a virago."

Laughter bubbled up inside her. "Oh, Francis, you look as if you mean it too!"

"I do." He sat forward again. "Pray do not look at me with such disbelief. On the one occasion I have so far seen her, she threw a shoe at my head. Oh, granted she thought me a lackey . . ."

Lady Clyde laughed even more. "A servant! You! Oh Francis, I cannot wait to meet her."

"You will be heartily sorry when you do, I vow," he warned darkly.

"Well, before I do pray tell me how I may help."

"You must take her up, of course. At seventeen she must needs be introduced into Society and then, my dear, we must hope and pray some poor fool is so enamoured of her he will take her off my hands before the mode of my life is utterly ruined. I could not endure the full eight years of guardianship and remain unbroken."

She laughed anew. "But if all you say is true . . ."

"It is."

"Then you are doing me no kindness."

He got up and went to her then, taking her hand in his. "You could not fail to transform her and to captivate her as you do me and countless others."

She gave him a mocking look. "And 'tis a wonder you do not charm her as you do every other female under ninety."

He chuckled as he let her hand go. "My fastidious nature would rebel against such a course. This is one female I have no mind to have fall in love with me."

"If she is female, Francis, she is bound to," Lady Clyde answered with a sigh, and then brightening, "I *must* go now, dearest. Didi was so very ill. Don't get into a pucker. Nothing can be as bad as you suppose."

Ushering her out of the room, Sir Francis was not so easily convinced.

Three

"Now remember, Robyn, you must make an effort to be civil to Sir Francis whenever you chance to meet. He really is so charming and concerned for you."

Robyn Wentworth was prowling restlessly around her drawing room, but even she could find no fault with their new suite of rooms which had Turkey carpets on the floor, silk covered furniture and a pleasant aspect of the garden at the rear of the house.

"I have no intention of being anything other than myself," she declared.

"I own your first encounter was unfortunate, but Sir Francis was not at fault and he did not look for this responsibility. If anyone is at fault—loath as I am to say so—it is Colonel Wentworth."

"I did not seek to come here either and would as lief return to Ropesby right now," the girl answered as if she hadn't heard her relative speak at all.

"But it is an excellent opportunity for you. You will meet young people of your own age—something you have missed up until now."

"I am happy with my own company, Aunt Lizzie. I have no use for vapid Society misses, or painted fops."

"You cannot class Sir Francis as one of *them*," Mrs Fordingbridge pointed out.

"He is far, far worse," Robyn murmured heatedly beneath her breath.

"You must make an effort to like him . . ."

Robyn turned to her relative. "Aunt Lizzie, do you remember anything of the time my parents spent in London before I was born?"

"I am afraid not, dear. My own stay happened several years before that. When your Mama and Papa were first married, I was already living in Sussex."

When someone knocked on the door Robyn went herself to fling it open. The footman bowed before saying, "Sir Francis presents his compliments and requests your presence in the library, Madam."

"Tell Sir Francis I am indisposed."

"No! Do not!" Mrs Fordingbridge cried before

the man could go. "Robyn you really cannot do this, you know."

"I will not be ordered around like a servant," she answered in a careless tone.

Mrs Fordingbridge snatched up Robyn's shawl and hurried towards her, saying, "Now, now, dear, that is not true. Sir Francis *requests* you to join him, and a great honour it is too."

The girl looked sceptical but allowed Mrs Fordingbridge to drape the shawl about her shoulders. "Come dear, let us see what Sir Francis wants of us."

"Oh, by all means let's!" Robyn retorted as she flounced out of the room.

She and Mrs Fordingbridge followed the footman downstairs to the small drawing room where he opened the door. As they entered the room they were confronted by the sight of Sir Francis in conversation with a most beautiful lady. Robyn glared at them both resentfully as they paused and looked round. Sir Francis came forward but Robyn did not heed him; she continued to stare at Lady Clyde who was as always dressed exquisitely in the height of fashion.

"Ah, Mrs Fordingbridge, Miss Wentworth, allow me to introduce Lady Clyde."

Mrs Fordingbridge dropped a curtsey and when Robyn continued to stare, her relative nudged her and she curtseyed reluctantly.

Lady Clyde got to her feet, saying warmly, "I am so very glad to meet you both. Do come over here and sit by me."

All the while Robyn studiously avoided even looking at Sir Francis who said in a serious tone of voice, "Miss Wentworth, you appear recovered from your headache."

She looked up in alarm then. "My . . .?"

"Last night when you were obliged to cry off."

She cast her aunt a cold look. "I am quite robust, I thank you, Sir Francis. I do not usually suffer the headache."

He smiled at that. "So I am given to understand."

Lady Clyde patted her hand. "I believe you are new to London, but I was acquainted with your mother and hope to know you better." Robyn sat with her eyes downcast, aware of her guardian's scrutiny and Mrs Fordingbridge's anxiety. "No doubt you have not been in Town long enough to choose tradespeople for your patronage. I do hope you will allow me to introduce you to my mantuamaker and my milliner who, you may be certain, are of the best and will serve you well."

Robyn continued to say nothing but Mrs Fordingbridge quickly answered. "You are too kind, Lady Clyde. Robyn will be delighted to be guided by one so expert in such matters."

The marchioness looked at the girl appraisingly and all the while Sir Francis observed them, a faint smile on his lips.

"Tell me a little about yourself, my dear. Do you dance?"

When Robyn continued to maintain a stubborn silence Mrs Fordingbridge was quick to fill the ensuing silence. "Robyn dances tolerably well, my lady."

Lady Clyde smiled. "I am so pleased to hear you say so, ma'am. I am always reluctant to engage a dancing master, for young girls invariably tend to fall in love with them."

Robyn looked up then, speaking at last. "I assure you, Lady Clyde, you would not find me so foolish, but as Mrs Fordingbridge has already stated, I was taught the rudiments of dancing at school."

Lady Clyde's smile faded somewhat in the face of such an unequivocal answer from a girl of such tender years. "Quite so," she murmured, glancing at Sir Francis who quirked an ironic eyebrow in her direction. "I am certain you can also sing and play *tolerably* well."

"No one who has ever heard me sing would ever say so, but I do play the spinet with a degree of accomplishment. I do appreciate your concern in this direction, my lady," she added, directing a rarely sweet smile at the marchioness, "but I feel I must point out that I attended school in Heysham, not in the wilds of Africa."

Lady Clyde could only stare at the girl in astonishment for a moment or two before saying quickly, with a faint smile, "I have a full diary for the present, but the moment I have a free morning be certain I shall call and take you to make all necessary purchases. I know of a mercer's warehouse in the Strand where the most remarkable French silks can be had."

"I was never one to concern myself with such matters," Robyn told her, experiencing a great feeling of satisfaction.

Not the least deterred Lady Clyde replied, "I vow that you will change your mind presently, my dear. The shops in London are altogether ruinous to the purse."

She got to her feet and smiled at Sir Francis. "I have promised to call in on Arabella Buckly now that her confinement is over, so you must excuse me for the present." Bestowing a broad smile on the others she promised, "You will be hearing from me again before long."

When Sir Francis accompanied her towards the door she said in a low voice only he could hear, "Of course she has a ruinously sharp tongue but I am persuaded she will learn to curb it before long."

"Poor Virginia," he said with some amusement. "For once I believe you are out-manoeuvered."

"Fudge! She is really quite sweet. I am certain only shyness and fear has caused her to behave badly to you."

His eyebrows rose a fraction. "Shyness! My dear Virginia, I would give a great deal to think her shy."

Mrs Fordingbridge moved closer to Robyn who glared sullenly at Lady Clyde's retreating figure. "What a famous thing! You are being taken up by the Marchioness of Clyde!"

Robyn transferred her icy glare to her relative. "I feel it only fair to warn you I intend to allow no such thing." At Mrs Fordingbridge's astonished look she went on, "Do you imagine I would allow *his* mistress to take me up? They must think me green indeed."

Mrs Fordingbridge gasped and raised her lace-edged handkerchief to her lips whilst glancing worried to the door where Sir Francis and his cousin were making their farewells.

"Robyn, you must not talk so."

"It is a patently obvious truth."

"I cannot agree, but nevertheless it is not prudent to say what one thinks on every occasion."

"Oh, Aunt Lizzie," Robyn said with a world-weary sigh. "You cannot be so naive not to know such arrangements are contracted. Men have their mistresses and ladies their gallants. Sir Francis has never been one to hide his rakehell ways. In fact, in this instance I admire his taste. I understand he is most discerning where the ladies are concerned."

She spoke with a sneer and as Sir Francis came back into the room Robyn got to her feet and went past him, sketching the slightest curtsey.

Mrs Fordingbridge hurried after her, smiling at Sir Francis and saying, "So kind of Lady Clyde. So condescending of her to take this trouble."

Sir Francis watched them go and then, drawing a sigh, he prepared to go about his business, neglected because of the unwanted intrusion into his house.

"The view from Saint Paul's is certainly magnificent, is it not, Aunt Lizzie?" Robyn asked as she pulled off her bergere hat and handed it to the footman.

Her relative looked rather less enthusiastic about their outing.

"It was indeed interesting, but . . ."

As they hurried up the stairs Robyn went on, "I declare I could see as far as Kensington. It is possible to see Kensington village on a clear day, you know."

"Robyn, it is all very well, but Lady Clyde sent to say she was going to call for us and I really don't think it is quite the thing to be out."

"Tush. I have already told you I have no intention of being taken up by Lady Clyde or anyone else. If I am a hopeless rustic, Sir Francis will have to accept me as such. I will not be transformed into a Society miss to suit his purpose, and there is an end to it."

"I doubt if the matter can be dismissed so easily," her relative answered darkly. "Come, in any event we must change for dinner. I must confess I am most uneasy as to your guardian's reaction."

"Having done what he deems necessary he and Lady Clyde will give me no more thought from now on."

She smiled smugly at the notion but her face took on a look of dismay a few moment later when she discovered a maidservant in her room, filling a bath before the fire.

"What is this?" Robyn demanded imperiously.

The maid straightened up before she curtseyed, saying, "Me name's Ella, ma'am, and Mrs Maggs appointed me your personal maid."

Robyn drew herself up straight. "I did not request one."

"I believe it was Sir Francis who gave the order, ma'am."

"How thoughtful," Mrs Fordingbridge enthused as she came into the room. "Just what you will need, my dear."

"I trust you will find my services satisfactory, ma'am," Ella said shyly.

"There is no chance of that, my girl. I want no maid, I thank you. Remove that object," she ordered, indicating the bath with a wave of her hand, "and then be so kind as to remove yourself."

The girl's face took on a look of dismay. "But, ma'am . . ."

"Go!"

"Just one minute," Mrs Fordingbridge said, coming forward now. "You must have a personal maid, Robyn. It is necessary for all ladies."

The maid looked hopeful, Robyn stubborn. "I am not a lady and I will not have my life managed in this way. Go away, girl; do as you are bid."

"The bath, ma'am . . ."

"No doubt Sir Francis ordered you to prepare that for me too; well, I do not want to take a bath, but when I do I shall order one for myself!"

"Robyn, 'tis the fashion now, I believe, to take frequent baths."

"Oh, I am beyond all patience!"

Ignoring her relative's comment Robyn picked up the pail the maid had been using and flung it at the unfortunate servant. The water which had been lying at the bottom of the pail soaked the unfortunate girl, but having turned her back in her fury Robyn did not notice it despite the maid's cries of distress.

"Take that back to Mrs Maggs," Robyn cried and as the girl scurried away Mrs Fordingbridge let out a gasp of exasperation.

"Robyn, I am ashamed of you."

"Oh, she is a servant and in this household no doubt she is used to far worse abuse."

"I warn you you will infuriate Sir Francis with this behaviour."

The girl shrugged. "Do I care what he thinks? I assure you I do not." The fury was spent and Robyn was now coldly calm. "You are besotted by him, Aunt Lizzie. You must realise he is no better than we are. Now, please go and let me rest; I feel very tired." When the woman hesitated Robyn insisted, *"Please, Aunt Lizzie."*

"I will return when it is time for dinner."

"I do not want any."

She went to lie down on the bed and as Mrs Fordingbridge walked slowly to the door she said, "There are times, Robyn, when I despair of you."

Staring up at the ceiling the girl answered, "No more than I despair of myself."

Before her relative could say more she firmly closed her eyes and the woman knew there was nothing further she could say or do. As she left the room she felt totally inadequate to admonish the girl, a feeling she had experienced all too often in the past.

When Robyn opened her eyes once more it was to hear the sound of raised voices in the adjoining room—one raised voice in particular, that of Sir Francis Derringham. The anger she could detect in his tone gave her a feeling of pleasure; more than that, it was power.

She sat up straight and listened for a moment before she realised that he was berating Mrs Fordingbridge and that caused some of her satisfaction to fade.

As she flung open the door to their drawing room she heard him saying in a calm yet angry tone, "Madam, Miss Wentworth's behaviour beggars description. What occurred beneath my roof today can scarce be believed, but I had looked to you to maintain a certain standard. To be plain, I cannot conceive what you are doing, ma'am."

The woman clapped a handkerchief to her lips, speechless in the face of his eloquent anger. Robyn flung back the door to announce her own presence which caused Mrs Fordingbridge's eyes to open wider and her guardian to turn the full force of his black fury upon her.

"Pray do not apportion blame on Mrs Fordingbridge. I am beholden to no one."

"I must correct that assumption, Miss Wentworth. Whilst I am your legal guardian you are accountable to *me*."

Their eyes met challengingly and it was clear neither would give way. Then he moved away, touching the back of a chair before he turned on his heel to face her again.

"When someone like Lady Clyde condescends to extend her patronage to you, you will accept gladly. I am ashamed to learn you conspired to be out when she called today."

Her lips twisted into a scornful smile. "Conspired, Sir Francis? What a ridiculous assumption. I was merely fulfilling a prior engagement."

"You have none, and what you did is inexcusable. Moreover, I must insist that the maidservant appointed for your personal use will be allowed to serve you in the usual manner." He gave her a withering look. "You certainly need every iota of help you can get. I have already told you my servants are not accustomed to having objects thrown at them. It is the last time I shall say so. Is that understood, Miss Wentworth?"

"Oh, I am certain Robyn understands now," Mrs Fordingbridge cut in quickly. "She has been woefully ignorant of the ways of polite society."

"This has nothing to do with polite society," Sir Francis answered, still staring implacably at Robyn. "Listen to me carefully, Miss Wentworth, for I have no mind to speak of this again. I am fully aware of the trying time you have experienced of late, but that does not excuse wanton behaviour towards those who are not deserving of your spleen. I am also aware that Colonel Wentworth did nothing to discipline you as a child and that Mrs Fordingbridge however well-meaning is equally ineffectual, but you cannot run around London as you wish. There are conventions which must be obeyed and I certainly intend to make sure no dishonour is brought upon my household. I trust that you now understand what is expected of you. It is not so difficult."

By way of a reply she turned on her heel and went back into her room, feeling more than satisfied that he could do no more than express his anger in words. Moments later, however, her satisfaction evaporated when he followed her into the room.

As she swung round on her heel, he slammed the door closed behind him. "I did not dismiss you, Miss Wentworth."

Her eyes flashed with fury and hatred. "How dare you come into my private room, Sir Francis?"

"Nevertheless, you are living beneath *my* roof. Understand me, I will not suffer my life and my household to be disrupted by you."

"Unfortunately, we are obliged to tolerate each other, so do not make threats against me. Your presence here is totally improper."

"You have no notion of propriety, so that makes no odds."

As he advanced towards her she began to back away. "You cannot remain here alone with me."

"Can I not? Who will stop me? Mrs Fordingbridge? She is as impotent against me as she is with you."

"Very well," she conceded in a breathless voice as he continued to move closer, "I shall make my apologies to Lady Clyde if that pleases you, but I have no wish to be taken up by a person of her kind."

One eyebrow quirked upwards. "Oh, pray do tell me of what 'kind' you consider her, Miss Wentworth. I am most interested to know."

Aware of the irony in his voice, she stiffened. "I refuse to speak to you here, so please go. We shall continue this conversation at another time."

"We shall continue it now, and you have not answered my question." She remained silent and he went on, "Let me tell you, then. The Marchioness of Clyde is a lady in every sense of the word. Would that you may hope to emulate her."

"That I shall never do!" Robyn tossed back her head in a gesture of defiance. "Oh, I do understand your zeal in espousing her qualities, although you may be said to be a trifle biased in her favour. No doubt you are equally fond of the serving wench you attempted to foist upon me."

"You really do need teaching a sharp lesson, my girl, and I am beginning to believe I am the one to do it."

She backed away even further, frightened now, for despite his calmness there was a steely look in his eye which she did not like.

"Pray remain where you are, Sir Francis," she told him breathlessly as she reached the bed.

She almost tripped over it, in fact, and was obliged to grip on to one post to steady herself.

"You are a spoiled, wilful brat, Robyn Wentworth," he went on, "and I will not suffer my friends to be insulted by a chit of your years, nor my servants to be maltreated."

He was far too close now for her liking and she quickly pulled off one slipper, hurling it at him with all her might. This time he did not duck; he caught it with remarkable dexterity and then he reached out to take hold of her.

"Don't dare to touch me!" she cried.

Smiling slightly he did not heed her. He caught hold of her arm and sitting down on the edge of the bed he pulled her across his knee. Robyn screamed as the slipper came down on her behind with a resounding thud. Half a dozen times more the slipper came down on her and all the while she screamed with pain and fury and struggled furiously to be free of his grip, in vain.

"Someone should have done that years ago," he said quietly as she was allowed to struggle to her feet at last.

Pushing her bedraggled curls from her tear-stained face she backed away. "Oh, you abominable man. All I have learned about you is true!"

"I doubt it," he answered without looking at her. He was smoothing down his coat. "But," he went on, eyeing her coldly, "you *will* learn that I mean to be obeyed when I say I will not suffer a hoyden beneath my roof. That at least I can teach you."

Her eyes blazed with fury. "All you can teach me is the way to Hell. If you dare touch my person ever again, Sir Francis, I vow I shall kill you!"

He shook his head. His very calm was provoking to her. "My dear girl, you do not learn quickly, do you?"

She flew at him with her fists clenched, but he merely caught them and before she had any chance to realise what he was about he had lifted her up and over his shoulder. He carried her, struggling and screaming to the drawing room where Mrs Fordingbridge was waiting, wide-eyed, jaw agape.

"Sir Francis!" she protested, "What are you doing?"

"Curing Miss Wentworth of the vapours, ma'am," he answered and with seemingly little effort he went out into the corridor.

Robyn's anguished cries brought many servants running to discover what was amiss and their concern turned to amusement at the sight of her being borne in such a manner. Sir Francis continued down the stairs and seemed not the least put out by her frantic struggling or cries for help.

He carried her to a part of the house she had not seen before, for since her arrival she had displayed a singular disinterest in her new home and certainly had no mind for exploration. As he flung open the door to one of the rooms Robyn momentarily stopped her struggling to lift her head. What she saw was a most remarkable sight which silenced her with surprise.

The room, with marble pillars and floor, was exactly like the Roman bathhouses she had seen portrayed in a book in Colonel Wentworth's library. Robyn had not believed they existed any more, but it seemed her guardian had indulged himself with the rare luxury of a modern reproduction. He carried her to the edge of the sunken bath where she recovered her surprise and renewed her struggles, pummeling him on the back.

"Let me go!"

"Very well," he replied in an even voice, and at last released his hold on her, allowing her to slip into the bath. Her eyes opened wide with horror as she realised what was about to happen. As she hit the water she screamed, gasping and struggling to keep her head above the surface. The water quickly soaked through her gown and petticoats to reach her skin. It cascaded down her face and her hair grew limp and heavy.

The shock momentarily silenced her cries, but as she wiped her face with her hands and tried to gather her heavy skirts about her she found it impossible to climb out. It was very undignified and there was nothing she could do about it. As her guardian moved back towards the door she gasped and shook the water from her face again.

"You can't just leave me here!" she cried.

He bowed to her briefly, not the least breathless from the effort of carrying her. "The temptation is overwhelming, but I shall send your maid to help you from the bath."

As he went out of the room Robyn stared at

him in astonishment and when he had gone she allowed herself to sink back into the water and cried out loud in anger and humiliation as the wetness lapped over and about her.

Four

Mrs Fordingbridge came hesitantly into the drawing room, bearing a small white card in her hand. "Lady Clyde is here, my dear," she said, a mite fearfully.

Robyn looked up to reveal a face totally devoid of expression. "Does she wish to come up?"

"No dear, she wishes you to join her in her carriage . . ."

Immediately Robyn put down her sewing and reached for her hat and gloves, answering dully, "I shall go down immediately."

The older woman showed visible relief. "That is so sensible, Robyn dear. Lady Clyde can do so much for you. I did so hope you would no longer resist your guardian's plans for you."

Robyn's face contorted at the mention of that

man, and the memory of the way he had humiliated her so.

"As we are forced to live beneath his roof it is as well that I do not. I would not for anything have him heap disapprobation on *your* head, Aunt Lizzie. This is something I cannot allow on my account." The woman had no time to voice her gladness at this change of heart before Robyn went on, "But even though I may outwardly obey his wishes my feelings have in no way altered. In fact, my hatred of that man has deepened and I vow he will one day curse my very name."

Pulling on her gloves she hurried from the room, followed by Mrs Fordingbridge who was looking rather perturbed at so dramatic a statement. "What do you mean? What do you intend to do?"

"In truth, Aunt Lizzie, I do not know as yet, but I shall not forget the way I have been treated, although I am only another in the long line of females ill-used by that man. If you intend to accompany us, should you not fetch your hat and prelisse?"

Mrs Fordingbridge drew back, smiling uncertainly. "Lady Clyde is to take you to her mantua-maker and various other tradespeople; you have no need of me. I believe I would enjoy the opportunity to lie down until you return."

Robyn's fierce expression softened and she

kissed her relative on the cheek. "Yes, by all means do so. You deserve a rest from my company." The woman began to protest laughingly and Robyn went on, "Oh, I know I am and always have been a sore trial to you, and although I regret it, I cannot help myself. There is a devil inside me which I cannot control. Perchance I have inherited such a trait from my father."

Mrs Fordingbridge laughed disparagingly. "Such nonsense, Robyn! Colonel Wentworth was never so wild."

Robyn bit her lip and then patted the woman's hand. "I will be good for the while. Have no fear."

As she hurried down the wide flight of stairs Mrs Fordingbridge watched her go, drawing a sigh. Then as Robyn went out to join Lady Clyde in her carriage she hurried back to her room.

As Lady Clyde's elegant town carriage moved out into Piccadilly she beamed at Robyn who sat opposite her. "I am so pleased there was no misunderstanding this time, my dear, and you are free to accompany me. You look very lovely today."

"I am a dowd and a rustic, Lady Clyde. You must not pretend otherwise."

The marchioness laughed, not the least put out by Robyn's frankness. She merely stroked

Didi who sat in her lap eyeing Robyn with disfavour.

"Your clothes are of no consequence—that can soon be remedied—but you do have the makings of a real Beauty."

Robyn averted her face. "Do I put you in mind of my mother, Lady Clyde?"

For a moment the marchioness did not answer, but then she said, "I did not know your Mama very well, my dear, but I do recall she had fair colouring whereas you are dark. I fancy you favour your father more."

Robyn smiled faintly. "Yes, I am persuaded that is true." Then, "I am given to believe my mother had many gallants eager to court her favour."

"Oh, too many to count," Lady Clyde answered before going on quickly. "Firstly we must see that you are clothed properly and then when that is achieved you will be able to make your debut in Society."

Robyn sat upright against the squabs, staring in front of her, displaying no interest in the sights beyond the carriage as any newcomer to London might do and taking scant note of what Lady Clyde was saying.

The woman looked at her with interest, at the ill-fitting black gown, hastily dried out after its soaking, the dowdy bergere hat and darned gloves.

"Mourning is so limiting, which is a pity. I feel that black is not your most flattering colour."

Robyn returned her attention to Lady Clyde at last. "It was not my choice, Lady Clyde. Aunt Lizzie—Mrs Fordingbridge—thought it proper, but I feel I have mourned for long enough."

"Well, providing we do not choose colours of too bright a hue we shall contrive handsomely, I am certain. The notion of presenting you, my dear, is quite exciting. I feel that you are bound to cause a sensation."

Robyn was moved to smile for the first time. "It is like that I shall."

"There is a deal for you to see and do, you know, quite apart from routs and balls. I am certain you will find the Zoo and the Tower most diverting, and then there is the Museum at Bloomsbury, not to mention the Royal Academy at Somerset House which puts me in mind of Sir Joshua. I will prevail upon Sir Francis to request him to paint your portrait. He is an old friend of the Derringhams, so I am certain he will agree. Sir Joshua Reynolds is the one painter who could do you justice, my dear, although Mr Romney who painted *my* portrait last Season is also very good."

At the mention of her guardian's name Robyn's spirits sank again. She had not clapped eyes on him since the day of her humiliation, something for which she was glad. The very thought of him was sufficient to send her into a rage. He was very rarely at home, although this did not surprise her. She had attended school with the daughters of several aristocrats and knew very well how their lives were spent in Town. Gentlemen gambled, drank and made love to other men's wives and ladies, once wed, spent their day in similar pursuits. To Robyn it was all unspeakably hyprocritical.

"You and Sir Francis are apparently close," Robyn said moments later, looking at Lady Clyde with sudden interest.

The marchioness smiled gently and her eyes were soft, something the girl did not miss. "Oh yes, indeed. I am exceeding fond of him."

Robyn, looking at the woman for the first time with real interest, could not quarrel with his taste. Lady Clyde was indeed a Beauty and dressed in green velvet with her hair curled and powdered beneath a large hat, Robyn felt that she must be a woman much pursued by gentlemen.

"How long have you been his *chère amie?*"

At this the marchioness looked shocked. "My dear Miss Wentworth, you are very plain-spoken."

"It is a country habit."

"You are now in London and I must warn you it will not do."

The girl lowered her eyes to feign regret. "I beg your pardon, ma'am."

"You do not offend me, my dear, but there are many who would be and you must court approval until you are entirely accepted."

"You must pardon my ignorance, for I was given to understand such matters were openly discussed."

Lady Clyde laughed deprecatingly. "Not *quite* so openly, my dear, and certainly not by girls of such tender years."

"I am much older than my years," Robyn informed her. "I have always had an independent spirit."

"So I perceive, but it is not always admired in a lady."

"I have never wished to be a lady. In Ropesby invariably I wore breeches and a shirt, and what is more I have seen mares give birth to foals in our stables, so I am not totally ignorant."

Lady Clyde hid her quivering lips behind her gloved hand. "No indeed, but of one fact you do seem to be ignorant, my dear; Sir Francis and I are *cousins*. His mother and mine were sisters."

Robyn was taken aback and could find no answer, so it was fortunate they arrived at that moment at the warehouse in the Strand. It was only as they entered the emporium that Robyn realised the Lady Clyde had avoided very neatly her original question.

At the sight of such a myriad selection of French and Chinese silks Robyn's mind was immediately diverted. No female however hostile could remain indifferent to such merchandise. Urged on by Lady Clyde and guided by her Robyn chose the materials which attracted her most, leaving her to feel slightly vexed at being tempted. But having been so persuaded to go against her own intentions Robyn felt that becoming part of the *beau monde* was now inevitable and it was useless to rail against it.

After they left the emporium, Lady Clyde whisked her to Bond Street to her own mantua-maker who measured and draped and clucked over Robyn's figure which was slim and yet shapely. Hats were chosen to match the gowns, fur tippets and pelisses were added to the shopping lists, gloves and shoes. When at last she entered Lady Clyde's carriage to return to Albemarle Street, Robyn felt exhausted. Her head reeled with all they had done and yet within her was the beginning of the pleasurable anticipation of being seen abroad wearing them.

"You will be able to take your place at any gathering now," the marchioness promised, looking pleased. "And there will be any number of invitations arriving at Albemarle Street before long. News of your arrival has spread around the Town and I do not have to tell you how anxious everyone is to make your acquaintance."

"Why?" Robyn asked unequivocally.

The other woman laughed in bewilderment. "Simply because you are a new face. All we have ordered today will be delivered in no more than a few days. I have made certain of it."

"You are very good, Lady Clyde," Robyn murmured.

"I am enjoying myself exceedingly."

"And," Robyn could not help but add in a mischievous tone, "at the same time relieving Sir Francis of my onerous presence."

At this Lady Clyde looked embarrassed. "You must not imagine that is how he considers you, Miss Wentworth."

Robyn's lips curved into a smile. "Lady Clyde, I do not have to imagine it. He would be exceeding odd if he did welcome my presence."

The marchioness waved her hand carelessly in the air. "No doubt he will grow accustomed to his new role as guardian, just as you will become used to being his ward. He really is too young for such a responsibility, you know. Colonel Wentworth would have been better served choosing a man of his own age."

"But had he married Sir Francis could well have had a daughter of my age, could he not?"

This observation caused the other woman some amusement. "Had he married directly from the schoolroom, perhaps."

"Did he never wish to marry?"

"My dear," Lady Clyde answered, still laughing, "I really could not say."

"There is one thing about which I must give you a warning," she went on a moment later and Robyn looked at her expectantly. "There is a deal of danger in excessive gaming, so I do beg of you not to get gambling fever. I have witnessed the ruination of more people by deep gambling than by any amount of extravagance. Only last year an acquaintance of mine all but ruined her husband who was a wealthy man. Now they are forced to reside quietly in Brighton and cannot afford to have a Season in Town. Poor Phyllida. First she lost her pin money, then all her jewellery before finally poor Alfred—her husband—was obliged to pay her outstanding debts. As I said he was all but ruined as a result."

"I find it extraordinary that her husband was so indulgent as to oblige."

Lady Clyde looked shocked once more. "My dear, any gentleman would be honour bound to do so."

"Then she was fortunate to have a husband, was she not?"

The marchioness shrugged slightly. "Many a father has been put in a similar situation. It is much the same. Many a female has sent husband or father to the Jews merely on the turn of a card or dice. I do feel it prudent to mention it now although I am persuaded you are far too sensible ever to be in such an invidious position."

"You are quite correct, Lady Clyde. I do not think the diversions to which I am about to be introduced will be of any interest to me."

"That remains to be seen, my dear. I fancy you will soon change your mind."

Robyn felt suddenly relaxed and she settled into the squabs as the carriage rattled along. "I suppose I am very fortunate to have a man such as Sir Francis as my guardian."

"I would not quarrel with that supposition . . ."

"What I am referring to in particular is the fact that he is a hero, or so I am given to believe, unless the matter has been distorted out of all proportion as I understand is so often the case."

Lady Clyde became immediately concerned. "You need have no doubt about the veracity of that tale, Miss Wentworth. My cousin did indeed save the life of our King and in so doing endangered his own to a perilous degree, although it did happen several years ago and Sir Francis would as lief have the matter forgotten."

"Oh, that should not be allowed," Robyn said

sympathetically. "Do tell me about it; I am in a fever to know everything I can learn about my guardian."

Weaknesses as well as strength, she thought to herself.

"Sir Francis himself is always reluctant to speak of it. He concedes any loyal subject would have acted in the same way, but in my opinion 'tis not so. He placed himself in considerable danger in protecting his King."

Robyn did not really wish to hear a diatribe in favour of the man she hated so well, but having broached the subject in which she was interested she had no alternative now but to listen.

"It happened when the King was visiting the opera, did it not?" Robyn asked politely.

"At Covent Garden. Sir Francis was in attendance. His Majesty was just about to enter his carriage outside the theater when my cousin espied a man in the crowd drawing a pistol from the folds of his greatcoat. As the creature stepped forward Sir Francis did so too, struggling for possession of the weapon before any harm could be done. The King was hurried away by his attendants and the pistol discharged harmlessly into the air, although it could just as easily have killed Sir Francis!"

Robyn thought how satisfactory it would have been if that had been the result, but then decided not. One could not wreak revenge upon a dead man.

"What happened to the man?"

Lady Clyde shrugged. "Declared insane, I believe. As far as I recall he was confined to Bedlam."

"No doubt," Robyn said thoughtfully, "His Majesty rewarded Sir Francis well for his valour."

"Indeed he wished to do so, but Sir Francis would not allow it. He, as I have already told you, was only doing his duty."

"How admirable," Robyn answered in a muted tone, for it was not what she wished to hear.

Lady Clyde laughed. "Naturally King George did not like to remain in my cousin's debt, but as Sir Francis told His Majesty at the time, there may come a moment when he will be asked to discharge it, although I cannot truly conceive of a circumstance when it would be necessary. Ah, here we are."

The carriage trundled to a standstill and a footman came to pull down the steps.

"Do you intend to come in?" Robyn asked uncertainly.

"I think not," was the reply, "but we shall meet again soon." As Robyn was handed down Lady Clyde put her head out of the window, with some difficulty due to the size of her hat. "I shall send my hair dresser around to you, Miss

Wentworth. You may leave the matter of your hairstyle entirely in his hands. *Adieu!*"

The carriage set off before Robyn had any chance to reply. As it bowled down the street she drew a sigh and glanced up at the imposing edifice of her guardian's town house. She understood that he possessed a magnificent mansion in Buckinghamshire as well as several other minor estates, and didn't doubt that in due course she would visit each of them.

As she walked into the hall she suddenly recalled Lady Clyde's warning against the evils of excessive gambling. The warning had been entirely unnecessary but now the germ of an idea came into her mind. I could be the means to ruin the odious Francis Derringham.

Before the footman could take her hat and gloves a door opened and she stiffened as Sir Francis himself came out of the library. The smile which had come to her lips faded. She scarcely knew what to say to him after the manner of their last meeting and in a totally involuntary gesture stepped back. As she looked at him fearfully he gazed at her with no expression evident on his face for a few moments before he began to smile urbanely, something which caused anger to well up inside her again.

She could not and would not dismiss his brutal treatment of her however hard he attempted to coerce her forgetfulness. However, as quickly as the anger had risen she quelled it, having learned painfully that she must deal in a more subtle way with this man. That he was totally unlike any man she had ever met before was only another fact which vexed her.

"Miss Wentworth," he greeted her, "you are just returned I see."

As he came towards her it was all she could do not to flinch away from him, and to her further chagrin he took her gloved hand which he raised to his lips. The light pressure almost burned her and she snatched her hand away as quickly as she could, bearing in mind that several servants were in attendance and she had already given them sufficient grounds for gossip.

"Tell me all you have been doing," he invited, losing none of his aplomb, although Robyn detected a certain coldness had come into his eyes.

"As I have been with Lady Clyde, I am certain you must know what I have been doing."

"Time and money well-spent, Miss Wentworth, if you do not mind my saying so."

"I have no objection to the truth, Sir Francis. Never fear to be plain with me, if you will afford me the same facility."

"I note that, Miss Wentworth," he answered

dryly and then he continued to regard her carefully for a moment or two before saying, "As soon as your new gowns arrive you will be able to go abroad more freely and enjoy yourself. Before long, when you are involved in a great rush of activity, you will quite forget that you ever mourned for your life in Devonshire."

She gave a challenging look. "Whatever gave you to understand that I did, Sir Francis?"

His eyebrows rose a little. "Am I mistaken?"

"Indeed you are," she told him with relish.

Urbane as ever, he smiled, recovering well from his surprise. "Then I foresee no problems and I am persuaded the social whirl should suit you well. Invitations are already beginning to arrive for you. Before long you will be pursued by any number of young bucks anxious to persuade me to relinquish you to their care."

"If that is true, will permission be forthcoming, Sir Francis?"

"Naturally, if you wish it and providing that the young man in question is suitable."

Her eyes challenged his. "Suitable to you or to me, Sir Francis?"

He bowed slightly. "To us both, Miss Wentworth."

She drew in a sharp breath and her head came up in a proud gesture. "Then it is fitting you should know I have no wish to marry anyone, so do not seek to foist me off onto one of your lecherous cronies."

"Miss Wentworth," he went on in a voice like steel, "I would not do any one of them such a disservice. However," he went on, his voice softening a little, "I feel moved to say that is a strange pronouncement in one so young although I am certain before the month is out you will be pondering on which one of your suitors to choose."

"You do not know me well, but I can assure you I mean what I say and it is not a rash decision. I shall never marry however eligible the suitor *and whatever pressures are brought to bear upon me.*"

"As you are aware, Miss Wentworth, I am considerably taken aback by this admission. Apart from a very natural urge in young females, are you otherwise aware that you would be obliged to leave your affairs in my hands until you are twenty-five years of age?"

Aware of the heavy irony in his voice her gloved hands clenched into fists. "I do recognise the disadvantages of my decision but at least when I am of age I shall be free and independent of *everyone* which is more than will be the case if I marry!"

Turning on her heel she said, "I beg you excuse me; I wish to go to my room."

"No, I do not excuse you." She hesitated and

turned around again, her breast heaving with indignation, whereupon he came towards the stairs. "You seem troubled, Miss Wentworth," he said as he stepped forward. "I do hope I am not the cause. Whilst you are in my care I would prefer us to be friends. Now we have come to an understanding—as I am certain we have—it would be best if we enjoyed an amicable relationship."

Annoyed at his perception and his coolness she murmured, "After our last encounter, Sir Francis, how could I fail to understand? But an amicable relationship might be a trifle hard to conduct, I fear."

"Oh, I bear no malice towards you, Miss Wentworth. You need have no fears on that score." Almost choking with fury Robyn moved away, not trusting herself to be near him. His complacency was infuriating. "Do not resent my authority," he said sharply, arresting her again, "for I promise I shall not assert it unless you force me to."

With her silk skirts rustling she swept up the stairs, enraged in spite of her vow to remain calm and match her own wit to his. All her carefully laid plans crumbled to nothing whenever she was actually faced with him. Her only weapon was impotent anger, a poor cudgel when pitted against his quiet and yet firm authority.

When she reached the first floor balcony she

paused, unable to stop herself looking down into the hall. Sir Francis was still where she had left him, gazing up at her expressionlessly. Their eyes met momentarily, his equally implacable. Robyn shuddered with some unidentifiable emotion before she hurried along to her own room to be alone with her thoughts.

Five

Lady Clyde swept through the crowds in the grand salon of her Park Lane house, smiling greetings to all her acquaintances. When she caught sight of Sir Francis Derringham, looking distinguished in his plain evening coat, she moved purposefully towards him.

"Francis, I had given you up this evening."

"I would hope you, of all people, would never do that, Virginia." He glanced around the crowded room. "It looks to be quite a hurricane, my dear."

"I would not consider one of my social events a success if it were not. Have you seen Miss Wentworth as yet?"

He glanced about the room again. "No, although I am aware of her presence. Several people have told me how charming they find her. Tell me, Virginia, why is it I cannot perceive her charm?"

The marchioness laughed as she fanned herself furiously. "Quite simply because she does not choose to extend it to you. You are not a person; you are her guardian."

He sighed as he answered. "I wonder what wickedness on my part rendered me deserving of Miss Wentworth."

His cousin chuckled. "I have no time now to enumerate them."

"I had thought you my friend."

"So I am. Only a friend could speak to you thus." She continued to flutter her fan and then glanced at him over it. "I believe you are too hard on the child. Mrs Foldingbridge told me what you did to her for being out when I called."

"It was a deliberate snub."

"Nevertheless you were too harsh, and moreover I am surprised at you for such a lack of control."

He looked momentarily vexed. "I was out of patience with her and understandably so. It was not merely her disrespect towards you which prompted it; she tossed a pail of water at a serving wench who was only obeying my housekeeper's orders."

"I cannot dispute the wrongs of that, Francis, and I'll warrant Miss Wentworth is as aware of it as you, but she will not easily forgive you."

78

He took a pinch of snuff before saying, "Perchance she will not, but she learned that I mean to be obeyed. She has made her debut and has entered Society, which she had up until then refused to do."

"She does seem to be enjoying herself thoroughly, I must own, although she has a remarkable taste for the bizarre. When we visited the Tower a few days ago she was quite morbidly interested in the sword which beheaded Anne Boleyn!"

She shuddered eloquently and her cousin laughed. "My ward is a most uncommon chit."

Lady Clyde gazed across the room sombrely, tapping her fan against her lips. "She is also rather unhappy, I believe, Francis, and there lies the cause of all her troubles."

He drew another sigh. "That is most certainly true."

"Of course the loss of her father and . . .".

"I am persuaded that has nothing to do with it. The answer lies elsewhere. It is unnatural for a young girl to take no delight in a social life, or to eschew the idea of marriage, not to mention her irrational and entirely unwarranted dislike of *me*."

"That is indeed odd," Lady Clyde agreed, giving him a wry look. "But how can we be of help if we do not know what troubles her?"

"It is something I intend to discover," he

warned darkly, catching sight of his ward at last.

He gazed at her for a while and she gave the appearance of enjoying herself hugely. Wearing a polonaise gown of lilac lustring with brussels lace in a fischu across her bosom, it did, nevertheless, display a great deal of snowy white flesh against which her mother's pearls nestled. Her hair had been curled and powdered and piled high amidst a miscellany of feathers by Lady Clyde's coiffeur, leaving her shoulders bare. The majority of Lady Clyde's guests declared her to be quite handsome.

"I note she is happy in the company of Captain Blackwell," he commented when he returned his attention to the marchioness who nodded her agreement.

"They seem to have formed an attachment. He is often to be found at her side."

"Of all the men in London I might have guessed she would form an attachment to the most unsuitable," he lamented. "I'll wager she does not know he is pursued by the duns and his discharge from the army was far from an honourable one, but if she did she would encourage him all the more."

"Oh, Francis, you are too hard on the girl. It means nothing. There are many men who are interested in your ward."

"Ah, but is Miss Wentworth interested in

them? I fear Captain Blackwell might be very much to her taste."

"Stuff and nonsense! See how many others are close by. It is not mere chance. She has the makings of a Beauty although not so much as her mother."

"Robyn Wentworth is not so vapid as her mother."

Lady Clyde gave him a surprised look before saying, "And unlike her mother, Miss Wentworth has taken to gaming with great relish."

"So I am aware. Only yesterday I was obliged to retrieve several vouchers she had issued."

"That is disturbing, Francis, especially as I made particular mention of the dangers of playing deep."

A light came into his eyes. "Well then, my dear Virginia, her sudden passion for the game is explained." At her look of surprise he went on, "Nothing could be calculated more to spur her on to anything than a warning against it. However, I am persuaded the novelty will soon pall, but before it does Miss Wentworth could lose a fortune. Let us hope she does not wish to emulate the Duchess of Devonshire."

"La! 'Tis true. Dear Georgiana must have lost ten thousand guineas tonight, but somehow I cannot see Miss Wentworth behaving so foolishly. For all your scathing opinion of her I suspect she is quite sensible."

The only answer Sir Francis gave was the raising of one ironic eyebrow and moments later he took his leave of her, wandering around the room in search of acquaintances, of whom there were many present. Eventually he espied Mrs Fordingbridge who had been sitting insignificantly in a corner until his recognition of her caused the lady to approach.

She smiled and became flustered as he addressed her in his customary charming manner. "I trust you find the evening enjoyable, ma'am."

"Oh, indeed, Sir Francis. How kind of you to ask! Lady Clyde is a most expert hostess." As he was about to move on she added, "I trust you have noted the change in Robyn of late. She has become quite demure and I am certain that is due to your influence in no small measure."

"It gratifies me that you should think so, ma'am, for Lady Clyde has only just scolded me for my severity towards my ward."

The woman became flustered again. "Well, I am sure I thought so too, but your method appears to have succeeded where so many others have failed. She has become a credit to us all."

"Indeed," he answered, feeling not in the least convinced of the miracle others would have him believe.

He was reminded of a youthful visit to the West Indies where the most ferocious of storms were invariably preceded by periods of halcyon calm.

As he took his leave of Mrs Fordingbridge he was accosted almost immediately by a foppish gentleman by the name of Lord Durley.

"Ah, Derringham," the man greeted him. "Just the person I wished to see."

"I am honoured," Sir Francis answered blandly, eyeing disparagingly the fellow in his brocade coat decorated by huge mother of pearl buttons and a profusion of gold chains and fobs. "How may I be of service to you?"

"I mean to be of service to *you,* Sir Francis. I have Miss Wentworth's vouchers for some ten thousand guineas, which I am certain you would as leif have in your possession."

Sir Francis eyed the man coldly. "I beg your pardon."

"Your ward, Derringham, has just lost ten thousand guineas to me in a game of faro. I deemed it prudent that you should know before I am obliged to redeem them elsewhere, for I am sadly out of funds at this present time."

Sir Francis successfully controlled his anger before saying, "You are not particular from whom you take your winnings—even green girls of no more than seventeen years."

The man laughed, ignoring the baronet's sarcasm. "Your ward, Derringham, is certainly not green. In fact, I am impressed by her maturity. She has her guardian's partiality for gaming, but, however, not his luck."

"If you care to step outside, I shall honour the vouchers immediately."

"Ah, splendid, Derringham. It is after all a paltry sum and I knew in accepting Miss Wentworth's vouchers I would be dealing with a man of honour."

"Ah, if only it were my fate to do so too," Sir Francis murmured as they left the room.

Not far away Robyn turned to smile at the man at her side as they moved from the faro table. "I fear, Captain Blackwell, I have played too deep on this occasion."

He gazed at her admiringly. "There are few of us who do not exceed our self-imposed limits on certain occasions, but my dear Miss Wentworth, this is not one of them. Do not let it trouble your head for it was not a great sum by any standards."

"I do not think my guardian will consider it thus," she answered not without a feeling of satisfaction. At this rate, she had decided, she would soon gamble away her own fortune, which meant nothing to her, and then Sir Francis would be obliged to use up his own.

"You need only to smile at him, Miss Wentworth, and he will forget any scold he would otherwise give."

She laughed gaily. "Oh, Captain Blackwell,

you must not confuse my guardian with lesser men."

"It is generally known that Sir Francis Derringham is receptive to feminine guile. Women have always been his weakness and it is one you must learn to exploit.

"You must also know that every gentleman honoured to make your acquaintance is delighted Fate consigned you to London Society. You are quite out of the common, and if only I could aspire to pay you court I would be the happiest of men."

"Why should you not?" she asked fluttering her fan in the flirtatious way she had emulated from others.

"Miss Wentworth, I am an ex-Captain of Dragoons not a man of means. I have little to offer one as illustrious as yourself."

Robyn smiled tightly. "Captain Blackwell, you are a fine figure of a man and have served your country well. I can think of nothing more noble than that."

"I confess I served my country as well as I could, although I was never able personally to save my King from death." Robyn laughed and he went on, "Although there are those who would say it might have been better for him to have failed in his valiant action . . ."

"Captain Blackwell, whatever do you mean?"

"Merely that there are many who still espouse the Stuart cause. The Hanoverian Kings are not truly ours."

Feeling acutely discomforted Robyn continued to flutter her fan. "I am not certain what you are saying is not treason, sir."

"Oh no, Miss Wentworth, a man is able to speak as he pleases in this country. If I disturb you when I voice the views of others, I apologise most humbly and hope it does not affect your opinion of my humble self."

She looked at him in amusement then. "How could it? You are a loyal soldier of the King and have served him well in your own way, I do not doubt. I am very impressed, if you must know."

He made a deep bow. "I am most honoured and shall continue to hope that one day I shall be worthy of your admiration and affection."

Robyn's amused smile faded as she saw her guardian approaching. "Blackwell," he said abruptly, giving the man only a cursory look.

"Your servant, Sir Francis," the man replied with a slight bow.

Sir Francis looked at Robyn, smiling pleasantly. "Much as I hate to interrupt an obvious enjoyable coze, may I have a few moments of your time, my dear?"

Robyn glanced uncertainly at Captain Blackwell before replying, "If you wish, Sir Francis."

He led the way out of the crowded salon,

saying, "Your gown is most becoming, Miss Wentworth. I applaud your taste."

"Lady Clyde was instrumental in choosing the material."

"Perchance she guided you a little, but I am convinced it is a result of your own good taste coming to the fore."

She glanced at him curiously as they came to a quiet corner of the hall where they could not be overheard.

"Sir Francis have you brought me out here just to applaud my choice of gown?"

From his pocket he withdrew a sheaf of notes she recognised all too well and involuntarily she steeled herself. "I have just now retrieved these from Lord Durley. You know, of course, what they are."

She nodded, less certain of herself now, and he went on, "These are not the only ones, as you well know. Since your debut I have been obliged to retrieve a staggering sum in respect of your losses. What do you say?"

She shrugged and eyed him over her fan. "Sir Francis, what would you have me say? I cannot deny what is undoubtedly true."

Eyeing her coldly he commented, "You are remarkably nonplussed."

"I am merely doing your bidding, Sir Francis, and participating in every diversion. Not to do so would be insulting to my hostess and I have no wish to be chastised on that score. I must admit, though, in forcing me to become part of the social scene you have done me a service which I readily acknowledge now; gaming is delightful."

"In future you will enjoy it from afar."

She drew back in alarm. "You cannot be serious."

"Do you doubt it?"

"I do not understand . . ."

"My dear girl, you cannot be so obtuse. In less than six months you could gamble away your entire fortune, and I would be failing in my duty if I allowed that to happen." He tore the vouchers into several pieces which he allowed to flutter to the floor. "There, that is an end to the matter and we will not speak of it again."

As he turned on his heel Robyn said, "And if I do not agree to stop?"

He hesitated and then turned to her again. "You would not be so foolish."

She smiled. "Neither would you disown my debts. You are trapped by your own code of honour, Sir Francis."

So saying she turned to go, certain that on this occasion she had enjoyed the last word. Before she had gone many yards, however, he had caught her arm and swung her round to face him once more.

"Understand well, miss, I have no intention of allowing you your head in this folly, and whilst we are speaking of such matters I do not much like Captain Blackwell."

"I did not suppose that you would, Sir Francis. Now kindly let go of my arm; I would like to try my hand at hazard this evening."

"If you do you will be very sorry."

"I think you can do nothing about it," she answered, for once looking him fully in the face, "save forbiding me to accept invitations, which would suit me very well."

He pulled her uncomfortably close to him. "There is a great deal I can do, make no mistake. If you insist on this course I shall have no alternative but to instruct every hostess that your losses will not be honoured. No one will accept your wagers then, Robyn, and be assured it is a very dire step, rarely taken. You will find the situation very humiliating and I shall not relish it either, so do us both a kindness in not forcing my hand in this matter."

He let her go at last and strode back to the grand salon leaving Robyn, her eyes sparkling with unshed tears of frustration and anger. She stamped her foot to alleviate some of her feelings and as she did so she saw Captain Blackwell approaching.

Although she deliberately turned her back on him, not wishing to speak with anyone at that moment, he came right up to her, gazing down at her sympathetically for a moment or two before saying, "I suspect Sir Francis has given you one of his set-downs."

"All for the sake of a few thousand pounds," she cried. "It is not to be borne."

"You suffer his strictures well, Miss Wentworth."

"Oh no, I do not," she said with emphasis.

"You must, of course, obey him, however unreasonable you regard him."

Captain Blackwell had merely confirmed what Robyn already knew. When she made no answer and continued to fume in silence he went on, "Such submissiveness becomes you ill."

"It would appear I must needs grow accustomed to it, Captain Blackwell."

"The problem is his control of your fortune," he murmured. "One cannot argue with such a fact."

"Until I am twenty-five."

"Oh, you will be wed before that."

"That, I am persuaded, would be an extreme remedy," she answered darkly, much to his surprise.

"Miss Wentworth, there are so many men who aspire to your hand. I doubt if you will remain unwed at the end of the Season."

"I advise you not to wager on that possibility," she told him as she restlessly paced to and fro. "There is not one of those fops I would have."

He gazed at her thoughtfully for a moment or two before smiling with satisfaction. "You delight me by saying so, but to hark back to your vexing problem, do not imagine all who gamble can afford to do so."

She gave him her full attention at last and he went on, "Believe me, Miss Wentworth, I do know what it is to be out of funds at the mercy of those without pity."

"I am not out of funds, Captain Blackwell, merely not in control of them as yet."

"The result is the same."

She could not argue with that. As they began to walk back towards the salon he said, "For ladies of spirit there are ways of augmenting pin money. Believe me, Miss Wentworth, since I left my regiment I have succeeded in living well on my wits alone."

She cast him a curious look but as they reached the crowded salon she caught sight of Sir Francis, in laughing conversation with a pair of beautiful ladies whose jewellery alone dazzled the eye. The sight of him, looking so nonchalant whilst she still smarted over their encounter cast all else out of her mind and anything Captain Blackwell might have been saying to her went unheard.

Six

Every part of the Drury Lane Theatre was thronged with elegant personages. The pit was crowded with young bucks who constantly jeered and called out to the players when they were not ogling the young ladies present in the boxes, much to Robyn's disgust, for she was enthralled to see the play itself. Unlike most of the others present, she was not much interested in the social aspect of the evening. The fact that ladies and gentlemen of great wealth and rank filled the tiers surrounding Lady Clyde's box did not impress her even though her own appearance was as imposing as that of anyone present.

All the ladies were fantastically gowned and bejewelled, hairstyles vied with one another in outrageousness whilst some of the dandies in the pit, in their towering toupees and exquisite coats covered with paste buttons, who for ever postured for attention, were scarcely less notable.

For Robyn the excitement of seeing the famous Mrs Robinson acting in *The School for Scandal* was everything to her. What amazed her was the fact that so few others present were interested in the proceedings, preferring to quiz one another or converse with members of the party.

As the curtain came down on the first half of the play, Robyn turned to Lady Clyde. "Is it not wonderful?"

The marchioness smiled indulgently. "Yes, dear, I must own that it is." She glanced at Mrs Fordingbridge who was dozing in the corner. "But I do not believe Mrs Fordingbridge agrees with our opinion."

Robyn laughed. "Dear Aunt Lizzie. You might think she would love this after rusticating for all those years. She is the one who was so enthusiastic about our coming to London."

"I expect she is quite done up after the hectic pace of the last few weeks. One of the penalties of a successful Season, I fear."

At that moment the lady in question awoke. "I remember Peg Woffington was all the rage when I was last in London," she said as if she had never dozed.

The others laughed, although Mrs Fordingbridge obviously could not appreciate the reason for all the merriment. The gentlemen of the party began to move out of the box—amongst them the Marquis of Clyde, a remarkably handsome and personable man, Robyn had discovered, something which had come as a surprise. She had always understood that the beautiful ladies of the *ton* married old men who would not interfere with their pursuit of love and pleasure. The Marquis of Clyde, it appeared, was an exception.

For once Robyn was enjoying herself hugely, as was usually the case when Sir Francis was not present. Whenever she was in his company, however, it was as if a blight had come over her life.

Suddenly she gasped as she caught sight of a party in an adjacent box. Eagerly she caught hold of Lady Clyde's sleeve just as she lifted her quizzing glass.

"Lady Clyde, only look over there!"

The marchioness did as she was bid and her lips curved into a smile. "How splendid. 'Tis the Prince of Wales."

"He is very handsome, is he not?"

"But rather wild I am given to understand. A natural trait in one of his age, but in a future king not very desirable."

"Is it true that he and Mrs Robinson . . .?"

"Oh yes, that is perfectly true, ever since he

saw her first in *Twelfth Night*. They exchanged *billets d'oux* using the names of Perdita and Florizel. All London is talking about it and I do not imagine the King is very pleased."

Robyn continued to stare across to the royal box until the arrival of several visitors, most of whom were admirers of either Lady Clyde or Robyn herself.

As Sir Francis had indicated his dislike of Captain Blackwell, Robyn gave him a particularly warm welcome.

"Mr Sheridan has excelled himself with this plan, don't you think?" she asked of him.

"I would not know, ma'am, for from the moment I clapped eyes on you tonight I have been unable to look at anyone or anything else."

She laughed and the marchioness said, "Miss Wentworth has a treat in store, Captain Blackwell, for she has not yet seen Mrs Siddons in her role of Ophelia or indeed Lady Macbeth."

"If Miss Wentworth were present, I should take no note of Mrs Siddons either, my lady."

The Prince has returned to his box, so it is like the performance is about to begin," Mrs Fordingbridge pointed out.

"Then I shall retire to gaze upon you, Miss Wentworth, from afar," Captain Blackwell announced. "This evening's performance will remain for ever in my mind and not for Mrs Robinson's acting ability either."

"That man is an impossible flatterer," Lady Clyde said when he had gone, not altogether approvingly.

"I like him," Robyn challenged.

"That is your privilege, my dear, although I feel bound to tell you he is not an acquaintance I would encourage."

Robyn was scarcely listening, for her gaze had come to rest on another of the boxes. Her eyes opened wide at the sight of Sir Francis Derringham, accompanied by a most beautiful lady. As their eyes met he inclined his head and his lips curved into the semblance of a smile at the sight of her astonishment. Moments later, angered by her own curiosity she turned away just as Lady Clyde caught sight of him too.

"Oh, there is Francis." She waved to him before saying, "It is too bad of him not to have called in on us during the interval."

"It looks very much as if he is well occupied," Robyn answered with heavy irony.

"I will brook no excuses," she declared.

"Who is the divine creature?" Mrs Fordingbridge asked, something Robyn had deliberately omitted to do, despite her overwhelming interest.

"Mrs Wilcox, ma'am. That is, in fact, her box. You will not have heard of her, I dare say, but she is known as the Queen of the Demi-Reps."

Mrs Fordingbridge looked aghast and Robin flicked out her fan before saying, "Sir Francis seems to have a partiality for royalty."

"Oh, bravo!" Lady Clyde applauded as they settled down to enjoy the second act.

Out of the corner of her eye Robyn could see Sir Francis sitting very close to the Cyprian, in laughing conversation for most of the time. After the triumphant ending of the play Lord and Lady Clyde's party made its way to the main entrance. As the theatre was filled with people of their acquaintance it was a slow progress but finally the door came into view with elegant carriages lining up to carry away their aristocratic passengers.

Robyn had enjoyed the evening far more than anything else in which she had participated since her arrival in London, and even her guardian's presence had done little to dampen her enthusiasm on this occasion.

"*I* recall an evening when Mr Garrick was an absolute triumph!" Mrs Fordingbridge was saying as they came down the stairs.

"So do I," Lady Clyde agreed. "On several occasions, in fact, including the night Clyde and I became betrothed. Do you recall Kitty Clive, Mrs Fordingbridge? I was but a girl in her heyday but the memory remains a cherished one."

"Yes, indeed. She never failed to reduce me to tears."

"What a pity Miss Wentworth is denied their genius, but you must both join me in my box again when Mrs Siddons appears at Drury Lane next."

"Oh, you are too kind," Mrs Fordingbridge murmured.

"It was always a dream of mine to become an actress," Robyn told them as Lady Clyde nodded and smiled at some friends.

She turned her attention to Robyn again, looking at her appraisingly. "That is an odd ambition, my dear, but in all honesty I must say I believe you would have succeeded handsomely too."

"Do not encourage her in this foolishness," Mrs Fordingbridge begged.

"She would have set London alight with her talent," the marquis added as he walked behind them.

Robyn blushed and his wife laughed. "Really, Frederick, I declare that is doing it too brown."

"I agree with Lord Clyde, my lady," one of Robyn's current admirers added.

Robyn laughed and fluttered her fan as the marchioness replied, "I dare say you are all quite right. I couldn't conceive of Miss Wentworth being anything other than out of the ordinary."

"You are all too kind," Robyn told them delightedly.

"Robyn was for ever dressing up whenever she was a child at home from the academy," Mrs Fordingbridge informed them.

"I always found it appealing to be able to escape into the guise of another person," Robyn admitted.

Lady Clyde gave her a speculative look before saying, "We occasionally have theatrical soirees at Clyde House—only in the spirit of fun I must own—but perchance on the next occasion you would honour us by participating."

Robyn's eyes grew wide. "You are gammoning me now."

"No indeed I am not. Frederick, tell her about our last effort. It was pronounced a great success by all who saw it."

Robyn's cheeks grew pink beneath the rouge Ella insisted she wear. The maid, Robyn was forced to admit, had proved to be very expert and a valuable asset now she was obliged to mix in the very highest circles.

" 'Tis true, Miss Wentworth," the marquis agreed. "My wife even transformed me into a lackey for the evening."

She laughed and admitted, "I should love to play in something like *The White Devil*."

At this Lady Clyde laughed heartily. "Oh, my dear, such melodrama would be a little too intense for our audience. Let me think on it and we shall speak of it again before long."

As the thought of actually acting in a play, albeit in Lady Clyde's drawing room, was an exciting one to Robyn, she fervently hoped the marchioness would not be long in considering the matter.

Lord Clyde left them to ascertain that their carriages were close by and as he did so Mrs Fordingbridge gave a cry. "Oh my goodness! Can that possibly be Rosamunde Lappington?"

Lady Clyde followed the direction of her gaze whilst Robyn's attention was captured by the young man at her side.

"That, Mrs Fordingbridge," Lady Clyde answered, "is Mrs Entwhistle."

"She was Rosamunde Lappington five and twenty years ago. How plump she has become. Ah, age rarely flatters any of us." Eagerly she went on, "We were bosom friends, you know, but then I married Mr Fordingbridge and we went to live in Sussex. I am sorry to say we lost touch with one another. Please excuse me, my lady, whilst I have words with her; she is bound to remember me."

Lady Clyde wandered away too, to speak to her great friend, Georgiana, Duchess of Devonshire, one of the more dazzling ladies of the *beau monde*.

As they wandered out of the theatre into the cool night air Robyn's companion confided, "Would that Lady Clyde puts on *Romeo and Juliet*. I would give anything to play Romeo to your Juliet. It would be divine, Miss Wentworth."

But Robyn was not listening to him. At the

head of the line of carriages, Sir Francis was handing Mrs Wilcox into hers. As he did so he caught sight of his ward and after a moment's hesitation came towards her.

Smiling urbanely, he bent his head over her hand which she withdrew as soon as she was able. He greeted the young man at her side who responded with a muted, "Good evening, sir," before withdrawing circumspectly.

"Lady Clyde is most annoyed that you did not visit us during the interval," Robyn told him before he had a chance to speak.

He looked surprised. "You were all so well-occupied I did not think my presence would be welcome. I shall entreat her forgiveness, you may be sure."

"No doubt when you join us at her house for supper."

He smiled. "Regrettable as it is, I have a prior engagement."

Robyn glanced across at Mrs Wilcox's waiting carriage, anger rising irrationally inside her.

"You caused quite a sensation tonight," he told her, "and not without reason, may I say?"

She looked at him again, snapping shut her fan. "That is quite an achievement seeing I am neither the mistress of a royal prince or," she added with some relish, "the doxy of every titled man in London."

Her guardian's face betrayed no shock or surprise, and as she stepped forward, recognising the carriage he had provided for her use it was he who handed her into it.

"Enjoy your supper, Miss Wentworth," he said blandly as she sank into the squabs. "I am sure you will with so many adoring *beaux* vying for your favour."

At that moment Mrs Fordingbridge came bustling up to the carriage and Robyn was glad to see her relative, for she had been on the point of uttering a sharp retort to her guardian.

"Oh, Sir Francis, I am so excited. I have just reacquainted myself with an old friend."

"A very happy circumstance," Sir Francis agreed, handing her too into the carriage.

Robyn continued to stare ahead, ignoring him completely. As the carriage set off she was aware of his continued scrutiny. As her relative excitedly chattered, Robyn could think of nothing except Sir Francis and her hatred of him which grew daily. Her opposition to his plans for her and her intention to ruin him by gambling, had been easily countered by him at a humiliating cost to herself.

Quite often she fancied she would like to have him murdered, but the thought ultimately gave her no satisfaction. But she was still determined to injure him in any way she could. Now she day-dreamed about triumphing over Sir Francis as a broken man.

The thought caused her to sigh with satisfaction as she sank back into the squabs. Old wrongs must be avenged.

Seven

Captain Blackwell came out of his lodgings in St. James' Street to be met by a crowd of his creditors. For once he made no attempt to avoid them. As they crowded forward waving their bills he drew out a purse.

"There you are gentlemen; enough to satisfy your needs, I believe."

As they greedily divided the gold, Captain Blackwell walked away, swinging his walking cane with a nonchalance he really did not feel. Although he had been late to his bed he had made sure he would be up and abroad early, for he had a purpose to fulfill. Those who were dunning him could be satisfied for the moment, but he had expensive tastes and a liking for gaming. He had always managed to survive his financial difficulties although he was aware the method he employed to do so was extremely hazardous and he wished to enjoy a more certain and safer income.

The answer to his dilemma was to take a wealthy wife but he had been frustrated in his efforts to do so. Since his discharge from the army he had paid court to many heiresses and rich widows, but his efforts had come to nought.

Now he could actually be glad of it, for he had met a woman, not only possessed of a fair fortune, but who was also very much to his taste. With Robyn Wentworth as his wife he would not only be a man of means but he would also be leg-shackled to a woman who was neither a vapid miss nor a raddled old hag.

As he walked towards Piccadilly, past postmen ringing their bells and the pedlars with their distinctive street cries, he smiled to himself, for Robyn Wentworth was a woman to whom he could actually enjoy being married. She was not in the usual style of Society miss but a woman of spirit and courage. What was even more important she had no taste to be in her guardian's power for a day longer than was necessary, and this was precisely the reason why he felt so hopeful. Robyn Wentworth would do anything to rid herself of her guardian's strictures, and what easier way of doing so than by marriage? The young man suspected that Sir Francis Derringham would be equally delighted to relinquish the burden of responsibility. Captain Blackwell had been quick to note that not only was Robyn and her guardian continually at odds, Sir Francis preferred to go his own way unencumbered, something in which the young man was only too happy to facilitate him.

All in all Franklyn Blackwell considered the Fates, for once, to be very much in his favour.

He arrived at the house in Albermarle Street in high spirits and presented his card to Sir Francis Derringham's house steward who disappeared for some while to return with bad news.

"I regret, sir, my master is still abed and cannot receive anyone."

Captain Blackwell was not in the least put out. "Pray return to Sir Francis and inform him it is a matter of the utmost import and I am willing to wait until he is free to grant me a few moments of his time."

It transpired that he was obliged to wait for almost an hour before a footman came to usher him upstairs. He was shown into the dressing room which adjoined the bedroom where Sir Francis was still in his dressing gown being shaven by his valet.

"Ah, Blackwell," he greeted him. "This matter must be of great import for you to be so willing to cool your heels for an hour."

"I would wait an eternity, Sir Francis, to achieve my heart's desire."

The baronet wiped his shaven chin with a towel before waving away his valet and sitting up straight. "I take it this had no bearing on the matter of the vouchers I have held since our game of hazard a sen'night ago."

Franklyn Blackwell flushed slightly at the reminder of his debt. "You are correct. That matter is in hand and I shall be dealing with it in the very near future."

Sir Francis got to his feet and pushed his hands into the pockets of his dressing gown, staring hard at his visitor. "Am I to assume then that this visit is in some way connected with my ward, Miss Wentworth?"

"That is a correct assumption, Sir Francis. I am here to ask your permission to pay her court. In fact, sir, I would marry her as soon as you please."

"It is not as *I* please, Blackwell. Has my ward given you reason to hope?"

"She has always looked upon me in the most favourable way, although, naturally, I would not deem to discuss such a matter with her before gaining your approval. For my part I have never met a woman I would rather take as my wife."

Sir Francis gave him a sceptical look before reaching for his snuff-box and taking a pinch. The relevance of Sir Francis not offering the box to him did not escape the young suitor.

As Sir Francis snapped the lid shut after what seemed to be an interminable time, he said, "I regret I cannot sanction such a match."

Captain Blackwell stiffened with shock and indignation. "But Sir Francis . . ."

The baronet met his gaze with one of iciness. "Miss Wentworth is too young and too inexperienced to consider so great a step as matrimony at this stage. She has only just made her debut and cannot know to choose wisely just yet."

Fury at such a calm dismissal of his suit flamed in the young man's eyes but he retained a calm demeanor nonetheless.

"Perchance I may hope, Sir Francis. If I approach you again."

"I regret I cannot give you cause to hope, Blackwell. Miss Wentworth is an heiress and," he added with a slight smile, "a Beauty, whereas your expectations cannot be said to be sufficient for a lady of her elevation. In kindness I must exhort you to put all thoughts of such a match from your mind."

Through stiff lips Captain Blackwell said, "Perchance, Miss Wentworth herself might wish a say in the matter."

Sir Francis smiled faintly yet again. "Whatever she might say can be of no import. Mine is the final say. My servant will show you out."

Sir Francis seated himself in his chair again, indicating to his valet to recommence the shaving. Seething with impotent fury Captain Blackwell bowed and left the room. He retained his appearance of composure until he was outside in the street again, but then his face twisted into a mask of fury.

He paused long enough to stare back at the house and say under his breath, "Oh no, Sir Francis, yours is not the last word in this matter, I promise you."

"Aunt Lizzie, you cannot be serious!" Robyn said in amazement two days later. "An offer of marriage. If Captain Blackwell had offered for me I would be certain to know of it."

"I cannot see it being a Banbury Tale, my dear, especially as it was Lady Burndale who confided it to me. It appears that Captain Blackwell is telling everyone of his rejected suit."

"But Sir Francis could not possibly do such a thing without consulting *me* first."

Mrs Fordingbridge looked bland. "Why not, dear? He is fully entitled to reject or accept suitors on your behalf."

Robyn folded her arms. "Is he indeed?" she murmured under her breath.

"Personally I believe Captain Blackwell shabby for such an ungentlemanly confession. He is indicating by innuendo that Sir Francis is refusing all your suitors because he wishes to retain control of your fortune, and you know how easily such rumours are taken up. It is too bad."

Robyn became alert again. "Are you saying, Aunt Lizzie, that he has refused more than Captain Blackwell?"

With an air of innocence Mrs Fordingbridge replied, "Why yes, I believe that is so. Obviously, though, none of them were deemed suitable."

"That is not for Sir Francis to decide, Aunt Lizzie."

"But it is, dear. You can depend on there being truth in the matter."

Robyn could contain herself no longer. She marched towards the door. "That may be so, but I believe I would like to hear it from his own lips."

Mrs Fordingbridge looked shocked. "Oh no, dear. It is nothing for you to trouble your head about. We women are not looked upon to make such decisions."

As she reached the door of their sitting room Robyn gave her a look of disgust. "Aunt Lizzie, it is my future which is involved."

Mrs Fordingbridge, anticipating trouble, hurried over to her. "Robyn, you are too young to know what is involved. Allow Sir Francis, who is older and wiser, to decide what is best for you."

This last pronouncement was sufficient to send Robyn flying from the room, slamming the door behind her. She accosted the first servant she saw, a maid come to mend the fire in her guardian's apartment.

"Is Sir Francis in his rooms, girl?" she demanded.

After the maid had bobbed a startled curtsey, she answered, "No, ma'am."

"But he has not yet gone out?"

"I believe not, ma'am."

Robyn hurried down the stairs, the skirts and petticoats of her gown rustling as she almost ran. The footman on duty informed her that Sir Francis was not in the library, a place he was often to be found.

She was standing in the hall, her hands on her hips when she espied Wilkinson, Sir Francis's personal manservant, coming towards her.

"Wilkinson, where is your Master? I must have words with him without delay."

"Sir Francis is unable to see anyone at the moment, madam. However, I shall inform him of your wishes."

Irritably she brushed the man aside and strode off in the direction from which she had come.

"Madam," Wilkinson protested, following her a few paces.

She turned to him again. "I do appreciate that

Sir Francis does not wish to see me, but I advise you, Wilkinson, to go about your business or it will be the worse for you."

Shrugging slightly the man did as he was bid and, still fuming, Robyn turned to survey the array of doors which were facing her. The first two rooms she entered had furniture shrouded with Holland covers and obviously had been out of use for years, but then as she backed out of a third she heard his voice.

She hesitated, recognising the strains of a popular tune from *The Beggar's Opera* sung in a strong tenor voice which she did not doubt belonged to her guardian. Setting her face into a determined mask she rushed towards it, flinging open the door and hurling herself inside before slamming the door shut behind her.

Too late she realised her mistake as his voice faded into a surprised silence. Unthinkingly she had walked into his Roman bathhouse and he was sitting in the water, complacently smoking a clay pipe in the manner of a rustic.

Immediately Robyn turned on her heel, ready to flee the room, but she had taken only two steps when he said, "Now you have disturbed my bath do not leave, Miss Wentworth, especially as you seem to be in something of a pucker."

"Do you wonder? I have just learned that Captain Blackwell's offer was rejected by you out of hand without so much as a by-your-leave to *me*. Others too if rumour is to be believed."

"For once it is. Oh, do come closer if we are to talk, Miss Wentworth. If I am obliged to raise my voice in this fashion for much longer I shall be hoarse within minutes."

Hesitantly and still with her back towards him she edged closer. His laughter stung her into a greater fury.

"I would not have considered you so modest. I confess it is good to see it in you."

At this she turned on her heel to see him calmly smoking his pipe.

"How dare you refuse anyone out of hand without so much of a mention of it to me?"

He put down the pipe and looked at her with wide-eyed innocence. "Of course, I dare, Miss Wentworth. I am your guardian, remember. And did you not tell me not so very many weeks ago you had no intention ever of being wed? I am merely carrying out your wishes."

Despite all her intentions to remain calm she did stamp her foot on the floor, cold and damp as it was, and she felt foolish the moment she had done so.

"That is not the point, Sir Francis. You should have consulted me on a matter of such great import!"

He picked up the pipe again and took a few puffs. The smoke was aromatic and filled the air, mingling with the steam and the smell of perfume in the water.

"Consult you, Miss Wentworth? I was very much tempted to call him out for his presumption." In a milder tone he went on, "You need not worry your head, my dear; the few fortune hunters who have come up to scratch are not worthy of your consideration. If they are the best of those who would offer for you, then I consider your vow to remain a spinster a wise one."

"Oh, you are the most infuriating man I have ever met."

One eyebrow rose a fraction. "Do you really think so? Most people own that I am exceeding good-natured."

Goaded beyond anger at his complacency, almost without thinking she reached out for an ornament to throw at him, but as she did so he told her, "If you throw that thing at me, I will come out and toss *you* in the water, and as you know it is no idle threat."

He gave her a considering look for a moment or two before adding, "You look a trifle heated, Miss Wentworth. I think it wise to call in a physician. Doctor Humpleby is a good fellow. A physic and a blister will do you no end of good."

"I need no physician!"

"If you say so," he answered in doubt-filled tones.

"There is no cure for *you*, Sir Francis," she could not help but retort, something which caused him to laugh.

"Take heart, my dear, I have some cheering news for you, for I am to go to St Albans for a few days."

She stole a glance at him again and he went on, "You might be aware that I have an estate there and must needs attend to some matters of business which will wait no longer. You, my dear ward, will be free of my onerous presence for that time, although in all fairness to myself I do not feel I impose upon you too much." As she began to move away, he went on, "If you do change your decision on the matter of matrimony I beg that you tell me of it so I may bear it in mind if any future offers are made, but naturally I shall continue to exercise the utmost discretion on your behalf."

She turned to make some cutting remark when he began to get out of the bath, something which caused her to make a headlong dash for the door, pursued by his laughter.

Eight

It was with some embarrassment Robyn greeted Captain Blackwell on the next occasion that they met, which was on one of her regular rides in Hyde Park at the fashionable hour.

Robyn rarely travelled in a carriage as did so many other ladies; she was glad enough for the opportunity to ride one of her guardian's excellent horses which he had put at her disposal. Accompanied by a groom, she was soon surrounded by a host of admirers, none of whom made the slightest effect on her emotions.

Although she did not love Captain Blackwell, she felt he was a man of hidden depths and something about him both attracted and excited her. He was not of the same ilk as so many of the other young men of her acquaintance. Neither was Sir Francis, she was bound to admit, although she did her utmost not to think about him at all.

She smiled a mite stiffly as Captain Blackwell came towards her on foot. "Miss Wentworth, how fine you look and what a fortunate encounter. I have been looking to see you for several days."

"I am flattered."

"You must not be. I am honoured by your attention."

Her head came up proudly. "I understand you called to see my guardian at Albemarle Street."

"A disappointing visit, Miss Wentworth. My heart was broken, but I have rallied for I do believe I may have some small cause to hope. In any event Sir Francis has not forbidden us to meet."

Robyn laughed harshly as she steadied her restive mare. "I think Sir Francis must realise the futility of *that*, Captain Blackwell."

"One cannot entirely blame him rejecting suitors out of hand. It would be a rare man worthy of you, ma'am, but the attraction of retaining control of your affairs must be very apparent to a man as astute as he."

"Captain Blackwell, for your own well-being I would advise you to restrain yourself from making such a remark. Sir Francis would be entitled to call you out for it, and he is not a man to shrink from a confrontation."

The young man smiled. "I would welcome the opportunity of answering his call, for it would free you, would it not, of his strictures? I do not believe I could do you a greater service."

"There is nothing to say you would win," she pointed out, smiling slightly.

"It is a gamble I would gladly take if the prize was to be you, ma'am."

Robyn was at a total loss as to how to answer him, but then, recovering herself quickly, she said, "I would not for anything have such an event take place on my account."

Captain Blackwell smiled again. "I was merely funning, ma'am. Such a possibility would fill me with horror too, I assure you. My army days gave me my fill of death and suffering."

"Then I trust we shall hear no more mention of the matter."

He bowed. "It shall be as you wish. I intend to do everything in my power to retain your regard."

"It is as well my guardian is at St Albans for he would not have appreciated the *on-dits* currently circulating."

"I trust you are not offended, for I can assure you the *on-dits* are in no way of my making. I value your regard greatly and still live in hope."

"Naturally, you still retain my regard, Captain Blackwell. My concern is for you alone, I assure you."

The young man looked more than satisfied.

"Your guardian's absence from Town is explained, for I have not clapped eyes on him for days."

"He has business at St Albans but should have returned by the morrow. Pray excuse me now, Captain Blackwell, but I am becoming chilled."

He stepped back as the horse moved away and continued to stare after her, the smile fading from his face. When he at last walked away he was deep in thought.

As she rode on, Robyn could not understand why she had, in effect, championed her guardian, for she suspected Captain Blackwell could become a valued ally in her struggle against Sir Francis, but all thoughts of either man were cast from her mind at the sight of a package awaiting her on her return to Albemarle Street.

"Oh, Aunt Lizzie," she cried, stripping off her gloves. "Only see what Lady Clyde has sent—a copy of *Othello*. It could not please me more."

"Well, I own it is very good in her dear," commented Mrs Fordingbridge who had only just arrived home herself after an afternoon pleasantly spent playing whist with Mrs Entwhistle and her cronies, "but is there some significance in such a gift?"

"Oh, Aunt Lizzie, I am out of all patience with you! There is a note attached. *Do you think you can play Desdemona*? It is for a theatrical entertainment at her house."

The other woman's eyes grew wide. "La! I quite forgot. How gracious of her to consider *you*. Desdemona. 'Tis the leading part."

Robyn's eyes shone. "Indeed! And one I could not like better. Poor Desdemona. So innocent, so wronged. I shall enjoy it exceedingly."

Her relative suddenly looked troubled. "You do not suppose Sir Francis would object?"

Robyn was angry that her guardian should be mentioned at a time of such pleasure and she said irritably, "Oh tush, Aunt Lizzie! Such entertainments are all the crack now. Even Her Grace, the Duchess of Devonshire played a maid in *As You Like It*. Besides," she added slyly, "he is not like to complain at anything in which Lady Clyde has a hand."

Reassured Mrs Fordingbridge asked, "Who is like to play the Moor, I wonder?"

Robyn shrugged and hugged the package to her. "I really could not care. Lord Clyde, perchance. He has taken part in theatricals before." Suddenly a gleeful look came into her eye. "The part of Iago would suit Sir Francis perfectly, do you not think?"

Mrs Fordingbridge looked at her blankly for a moment or two before she laughed. "Oh, foolish child. As if Sir Francis would consent to act in a *play*. He has no wife to encourage him in such foolishness.

"Enough of this foolishness, dear. You are still in your riding habit and we must both change for dinner at the Garringtons. Your blue velvet gown is laid out and Ella is waiting to do your hair. Come along now; to be late would be inconceivable."

Robyn allowed herself to be hurried from the room although her mind was already formulating the best way she could play Shakespeare's hapless heroine.

Consequent to the arrival of the manuscript, Robyn found the evening not in the least enjoyable. The company was too staid for her liking and she was in a fever to begin learning her lines, although the play would not be performed in its entirety, merely the part of it where Othello pleads his love for Desdemona to Brabantio and the end where she and Othello die.

As soon as tea was served she contrived the complaint of a headache and she and Mrs Fordingbridge returned to Albemarle Street at a comparatively early hour.

"You must go straight to your bed," Mrs Fordingbridge told her as they entered the hall. "I will instruct a servant to make you a posset."

"There is no need to fuss, Aunt Lizzie. I am perfectly recovered now."

The other woman eyed her doubtfully. "You were exceeding quiet all evening, I noted."

"Only because I was devilishly bored. I had no headache, Aunt Lizzie. I am merely in a fidge to read *Othello*."

As Robyn started up the stairs Mrs Fordingbridge gave her a reproachful look. "I am disappointed in you. Lady Garrington has been exceeding kind to you."

"Oh, but Lord Garrington did insist on touching my leg beneath the table, and Viscount Wragg is such a cork-brained young man to be seated next to for an entire evening. I counted seven patches on his face and he uses civet perfume, which always makes me sneeze."

Mrs Fordingbridge sighed as she followed Robyn up the stairs. "I must agree that Viscount Wragg is too much of a daffy-down-dilly for your taste, my dear, and I cannot quarrel with your guardian's decision against Captain Blackwell, but is there no one for whom you would throw your cap over the windmill?"

At this Robyn was forced to laugh. "No, Aunt Lizzie, and it is fortunate that I do not have to."

"I have never heard such twaddle from a young girl. Most women would give anything for your advantages in that direction. You lack no suitors."

"That does not mean to say I shall accept one."

"But you truly cannot mean to remain a spinster."

"Why should I not? I need no man to provide me with pin money. Do I really need to marry a man who will be unfaithful as soon as I have put an heir into the nursery, leaving me with nothing to do save exchange *on-dits* and flirt with a succession of gallants?"

"My dear, what has given you such strange notions?"

She looked at the woman challengingly. "Tell me I am in error Aunt Lizzie."

She continued to stare at the woman who was the first to look away. Triumphant, Robyn turned on her heel and would have gone to her room if a commotion in the hall below had not caused her to draw back.

The front door had been thrown open to admit several grooms who were followed by Wilkinson, apparently in the strange role of supporting Sir Francis. Robyn leaned over the balustrade to obtain a better view of the remarkable scene.

"Dear me," gasped Mrs Fordingbridge, "I wonder what has happened."

"Damn you, Wilkinson!" Sir Francis cried. "Unhand me. I am not at death's door, you fool."

Robyn and her relative watched anxiously as Sir Francis made his unsteady way up the stairs, accompanied by a bevy of servants all intent upon helping him. His condition was truly amazing, for Robyn had never seen him other than immaculate.

"Sir Francis, what is amiss?" she asked when he reached the top of the stairs.

As he stared at her she noted a tear in his caped greatcoat and his hair hanging limply around his pale face. Clutching one arm as if it pained him he eyed her for a moment or two before answering.

"You look concerned, Miss Wentworth, for which I thank you. You will be glad to learn this encounter with a tobyman did not end with my death."

So saying, he went into his apartment, slamming the door on all but Wilkinson.

"Oh, heavens preserve us!" wailed Mrs Fordingbridge. "A highwayman. Poor Sir Francis. What a frightful experience."

"Yes, indeed," Robyn answered absently, then hurrying her relative away to her room. "He does not appear to be hurt, fortunately."

When Mrs Fordingbridge was settled for the night Robyn could not contain her curiosity and concern any longer and she returned to Sir Francis's apartment in time to see Wilkinson coming out.

"Wilkinson, how does Sir Francis? Has he been harmed?"

The man allowed a fleeting smile to cross his face. "It would appear he is in fine fettle, madam.

The wound is no more than a scratch after all—the ball missed him entirely and he will not allow a physician to be called. A poultice is all that is needed."

Robyn smiled uncertainly. "That is indeed a relief."

"To us all, madam. When I left Sir Francis was bemoaning the ruination of his greatcoat rather than the loss of his purse."

"Wilkinson, what actually happened tonight?"

"The carriage was travelling along the Edgeware Road when it was held up. 'Twas a miracle Sir Francis was not killed, madam; I tell no lie."

Her eyes clouded at the realisation that he might have died that night and she experienced nothing but pain.

"But that is dreadful. I scarce dare think of what might have transpired. Did the scoundrel escape?"

"Unfortunately, madam, he did, but I believe Sir Francis did wing him. He is a crack shot and always carries his own pistols concealed in the carriage although he did not draw them until he was himself attacked. If my opinion means anything, madam, I believe the scoundrel deliberately attempted to kill Sir Francis."

Robyn gasped. "You cannot be serious, Wilkinson."

"Indeed, I am, madam. Why else would he

fire upon Sir Francis even though he had already seized his purse?"

As he went down the corridor her horror-filled eyes followed him and then she stared at the closed door to her guardian's apartment before going slowly and thoughtfully back to her own room. It was a long time before she slept that night, although, for once, it was not because she raged with hatred at her guardian.

Nine

The following morning Robyn awoke early and after dressing quickly hurried along the corridor until she found a servant of whom she asked, "Is Sir Francis still confined to his rooms?"

"I believe not, madam," the lackey replied. "I understand Sir Francis is as usual in the library."

The news confirmed, at least, that he was quite recovered but Robyn was totally unprepared for the feeling of relief she experienced. Without giving it much consideration, she continued on her way and only when she reached the library doors did she pause to wonder how best she could voice her enquiry as to his health. She justified it in her own mind by telling herself Mrs Fordingbridge would expect it of her.

As the footman eyed her curiously a noise behind her made her turn on her heel in alarm. "Oh, you shocked me, Oswald," she said reproachfully at the sight of Lady Clyde's black page, resplendent in his brocade livery and turban.

"Sorry, madam," he said in a tone which belied the sentiment. He grinned at her, displaying an expanse of white teeth.

"What are you doing here?" she asked, eyeing Lady Clyde's dog which the page was holding.

"Didi doesn't like Sir Francis, and Sir Francis doesn't like him."

Robyn stiffened. "I am not surprised," she answered, eyeing the dog coldly. "I take it Lady Clyde is with Sir Francis."

"Yes, ma'am." Robyn was vexed that the marchioness had got there first, although she realised it was an irrational thought. The page looked all around him before saying in a hushed whisper, "They do say it was Captain Swell who held up Sir Francis last night."

Robyn began to move away, reconciled to not seeing her guardian after all. "I know nothing about the matter and I do not think Sir Francis would be pleased to know it is being discussed."

"Aren't you going to join them? Can't you bear to share him?"

"*You* are impudent and if you say another word I shall box your ears."

His eyes grew large and round. "No, ma'am. I'm not impudent; I am Oswald."

Her resentment at finding her guardian engaged with Lady Clyde faded and she could not help but smile at the boy's impudence.

"You are very close to your mistress, are you not, Oswald?"

"Yes, ma'am. There's a good deal I know about my lady."

"Why do you suppose she and Sir Francis never married?"

"Lady Clyde has a husband already," he answered simply.

"She didn't always."

"They are of the same family. White Quality don't like blood to mix."

Robyn sighed. "Yes, I suppose that is the answer, Oswald. It would also answer why Sir Francis has never wed. There can be no one in his eyes equal to Lady Clyde."

"That is certainly true, madam."

She looked at him coldly. "That will be enough, Oswald. You had better go back to your station outside the library. Lady Clyde will want Didi the moment she is finished her coze with Sir Francis."

"*Yes*, ma'am," the page answered with a grin, but this time he received no smile in return from Robyn.

* * *

"Are you quite certain you are not harmed, Francis," Lady Clyde demanded the moment she had been ushered into the library where her cousin had been going about his business as was usual at that time of the day.

He gave her a reassuring smile. "As you can see I am as robust as ever. I cannot understand what all the botheration is about."

She drew a sigh of relief and sank down into the chair he had pulled out for her. "I was quite overcome when I learned of it. My maid was obliged to burn feathers to revive me. Oh, it is too bad. Not a sen'night ago poor Lady Fothersgill lost her emeralds to a cut purse and Sir Donald Harpenden was robbed of his diamond buckles as well as his purse on Hounslow Heath. When I think what might have transpired I could swoon again, I declare. What damage has been done?"

"A mere scratch. My coat took the brunt of the ball. A new coat too. I am not too pleased about that you may be sure."

"Oh Francis," she said despairingly.

He put his hands on her shoulders. "You are a true friend, Virginia. Would that everyone could be so concerned for me."

"I can assure you that they are." She looked at him then with interest. "Do you have any particular person in mind?"

He walked away from her, moving towards

the desk. "The fellow was masked, done up in a great frieze coat too, so it was impossible for me to recognise him, and yet I had the feeling I knew him."

"Really?"

"He was not the usual scum of the road, Virginia. The horse was of the finest. Yes, I am certain he was a gentleman even though he contrived to disguise his voice."

"It is not unknown for gentlemen in dire straits to seek the blunt in such a way."

"No, indeed, that is precisely what occurred to me." He looked thoughtfully at an object on his desk before picking it up.

Lady Clyde said, "That is surely not your purse."

"Not the purse itself, that much I can say. To be precise this is payment of a debt. The money arrived by messenger this morning, sent by Captain Blackwell who lost to me at hazard some few weeks ago. As everyone knows Captain Blackwell is in dun territory—when is he not?—and I was most reluctant to accept his vouchers but he was so insistent I could not gainsay him without inviting the accusation that I had insulted him. The amount repaid here is exactly that stolen from me last night. You must own, Virginia, speculation on how he came by this considerable sum is inevitable."

"The notion of his being a highwayman has

never occurred to me, but I own it is possible. He is not a man to let his scruples stand in the way of his own advancement, but why should he invite speculation by sending you the purse this very morning?"

Sir Francis sat on the edge of his desk fingering the purse thoughtfully. "Because he is an arrogant popinjay who considers me a rum cull. I have no proof, so I can do nothing, something of which he must be well aware. The fact that he sent round this morning is no coincidence, I am sure. I am convinced he wishes me to know for certain that it was he."

"Impudent creature. What are you going to do about him?"

"There is precious little I *can* do, my dear, but I am not much dismayed by that; I am convinced that if he persists in this course he will eventually be caught and swing from the Tyburn Tree. The roads are well-patrolled these days, and he cannot escape justice for ever."

He glanced at his cousin. "Robyn has been much in his company of late, has she not?"

"Yes," she answered thoughtfully, "but I would not say she was enamoured of him. In fact, your ward, Francis, is remarkably resilient to those who pay court to her."

"Yes, I am aware of that, and yet she may have given Blackwell cause to think her in earnest, for he has made an offer, which I

134

naturally refused, moreover giving him no hope for the future.

"Virginia, that tobyman who held up my carriage, shot at me quite deliberately when I gave him no cause to do so. I truly believe that was the object of the robbery, not to gain possession of my purse."

Lady Clyde gasped at the implication of his words. "But if it was Captain Blackwell . . ."

"Yes, indeed," he answered heavily. "He just might think that if I were in my grave the way would be clear for him to marry Robyn. The chucklehead has no notion that she does not wish to marry anyone. She is merely using him to feed her own vanity—and my disapproval.

"What troubles me most is the fact that he knew where I would be," he went on thoughtfully, "so the question remains; did Blackwell act alone in his own interests, or did Miss Wentworth put him up to it?"

"Francis!"

He smiled in the face of her shock. "I do not regard it as an impossibility. She has a wild streak and an unreasoning hatred of me, and because she appears to conform with our wishes at this moment, does not mean she is tamed."

"How dramatic that sounds. She might rail at your authority, but she would never connive at your death. Have you discovered why she hates you so?"

"It is possible to hazard a guess; I am the first figure of authority she has ever encountered. Her father never was, and I believe the various academies she entered were only just able to cope. But I am not dismayed. At the moment she has windmills in her head but no doubt, despite an avowed spinsterhood, she will one day throw her cap over the windmill for some young buck, and I shall be done with her. However, when that does happen I fear it will not be a simple love affair—not with Miss Wentworth involved."

She laughed at his prediction. "That may well be true, but at least I am certain you can rest assured there is little that is bad in her whatever you may think. And now my mind is at ease about you, I must go."

He walked with her to the door. "What I have said to you about Blackwell is for our ears only, Virginia. I am certain you are sensible of that fact."

"You can rely upon my discretion," she answered, pulling on her gloves, "although how I shall be able to resist a shudder whenever I see him I cannot conceive."

"If he is innocent, it is of no consequence, and if not—well, tobymen are invariably caught and brought to justice. His pockets are always to let. He will need to take to the high toby again, you will see."

She gave him a concerned look. "And if it is true, are you not concerned that he . . . might make another attempt to harm you?"

He smiled reassuringly. "The opportunity will not easily arise again; whatever else Blackwell might be, he is not a hero."

"And Miss Wentworth is not so evil."

"I trust you may be right, Virginia."

Touching her hat to ascertain its pert angle she said, "Do not forget I have arranged my theatrical soiree. I would not have you miss it over this."

"This incident will not interfere with any of my activities, Virginia, and this one I would not miss for anything!"

Robyn decided she would seek Lady Clyde's advice on how best to approach her part as Desdemona, for she was viewing the coming soiree with as much seriousness as a professional actress regarded an appearance at Drury Lane.

Accompanied by Mrs Fordingbridge, Sir Francis's carriage took them to Park Lane, only for them to be told that the marchioness was not at home. Robyn was not really surprised as she was aware Lady Clyde led a very hectic social life, but she was disappointed nonetheless. Without being aware of the fact, she had been coming to rely on the marchioness's counsel more and more, although the one matter she might like to have discussed with her was impossible to broach with someone so close to Sir Francis.

"You will see her at Ranelagh this evening," Mrs Fordingbridge pointed out.

"But we shall not be able to discuss the play in detail. Lady Clyde, I regret to say, is not treating this matter as seriously as I believe she should. On the last occasion I spoke to her, she could not even tell me who the other actors would be."

"I suggest you leave a note and her ladyship may call on you at her convenience."

"Oh, it is really of no consequence, Aunt Lizzie," Robyn said with sudden impatience. "I am making too much of this. Lady Clyde has put on other soirees in the past and if it needs to be discussed no doubt we shall do so. I do not wish to be considered a rustic in this matter, so I shall not mention it again until it is spoken of to me."

She climbed back into the carriage, leaving her bewildered relative to follow. "Really, Robyn dear, I find your logic quite perplexing at times."

The girl laughed. "Do not let it trouble your head, Aunt Lizzie. I just do not wish to make a cake of myself."

As the carriage set off again she went on, "However, I *am* determined to perform as well as any professional when the evening arrives."

"I have rarely seen you in such a taking as over this attempt at theatricals."

Robin's eyes glowed. "Aunt Lizzie, that is because I have a notion. You know I have always enjoyed play-acting and I have now decided that when I am free of this despised guardianship I intend to go on the stage."

Not surprisingly Mrs Fordingbridge recoiled with shock. "Robyn!"

"Aunt Lizzie, do not look so shocked, I beseech you," she answered with a laugh. "I did not say I intended to enter a bawdy house, or, for that matter, a convent."

"You are outside of enough, Robyn. Whoever heard of a young lady with your prospects going on the stage?"

"Once I have reached the age of five and twenty there will be no one who can stop me doing anything I wish."

"There are times when I truly believe your attic's to let, my girl. Oh, I know you intend to remain unwed, but unless she is fit for Bedlam no female does that from choice."

"This one will, except in the event I meet a man so ineffectual he cannot influence me. If marriage to such a creature will free me of Sir

Francis before I reach five and twenty, I might yet consider it."

Mrs Fordingbridge looked out of the window. "I do not know what poor Sir Francis has done to earn your disapprobation."

"I pray that you never will," Robyn murmured beneath her breath.

A moment later her relative said, "I really must purchase some lace for my collar, and as I an going to sew some caps I must also needs buy muslin."

"That will not take long to do. Perchance we may ride in the Park on the way home."

Mrs. Fordingbridge beamed at the prospect of her relative suggesting so conventional a pastime. The woman still shuddered at the memory of their visit to the Surgeon's Hall to see the anatomical specimens on view there.

"My dear, I am persuaded that will be delightful, and may I also say how pleased I am at the change in you of late? In Ropesby I often dreamed of a Season in London for you, not truly believing it would ever be possible. You were so set against it, but only see how well it has transpired."

At the sight of Mrs Fordingbridge's pleasure, Robyn turned away, becoming more subdued at the reminder of how far she had conformed despite all her initial vows. However, it was only an outward display and she was still determined to make Sir Francis Derringham regret her existence.

Hyde Park was crowded with fashionables, not so much taking the air as displaying themselves. Elegant carriages made slow progress amongst the strollers and the horsemen, but no one was actually in any hurry. It was more important to see and be seen by one's friends. The carriage which Robyn and her chaperone occupied was often stopped by new acquaintances, some of whom were foppish young men who sought Robyn's favour.

When she saw Franklyn Blackwell approaching on his hack she ordered the driver to stop, smiling at the young man simply because she knew her guardian would not approve.

"Captain Blackwell, we have not seen you abroad of late," she said after he greeted both ladies warmly. "I do hope you have not taken me in dislike."

The young man looked shocked at the very thought. "Madam, no amount of ill-usage on your part would induce me to such a course. I am only honoured that you should find my absence noteworthy. I have, in fact, been obliged to be out of town on business for a while."

"Concluded satisfactorily, I trust?"

His hand unconsciously gripped his other arm. "I regret not." He smiled then. "However, it is of no account. My only concern is that no other man has taken my place in your heart."

She laughed. "As I am reputed to have no heart, Captain Blackwell, I doubt if that is possible."

"If you have no heart, ma'am, there are many who would be only too willing to give you theirs, myself included." He went on, looking more serious now, "I understand your guardian has recently suffered an unfortunate encounter, Miss Wentworth."

"More unfortunate for the scoundrel who attacked him," Mrs Fordingbridge answered. "Sir Francis insists *he* had the worst of it."

He smiled slightly. "That sounds very much like Sir Francis, but is it true?"

"That is something we cannot know," the woman answered.

Robyn laughed gaily again and Captain Blackwell asked, "I trust Sir Francis is quite recovered."

"Oh yes indeed," Robyn told him.

Captain Blackwell's fingers tightened on his riding whip. "The Fates were obviously in his favour. It is to be hoped Fortune continues to smile on him."

He inclined his head but as he gripped the reins to turn his horse a spasm of pain contorted his face.

Robyn leaned forward. "Captain Blackwell, is something amiss? You seem in some distress."

He recovered quickly and smiled at her in a reassuring manner. "It is nothing, ma'am, merely an old war wound which plagues me from time to time. Good day, ma'am, Mrs Fordingbridge."

He touched his hat and rode on. Mrs. Fordingbridge instructed the driver to move off as Robyn sank back into the squabs.

"His tongue is well hung, I do admit." She glanced at Robyn. "I have the feeling, though, he is not at all displeased at poor Sir Francis's encounter and misfortune."

Robyn smiled. "I am sure that he was not, nor would I expect him to be."

The answer to where Lady Clyde had been at the time they called at Clyde House was soon revealed. As the carriage continued on its frequently interrupted way, Robyn caught sight of a high-perch phaeton making its way towards them.

The carriage itself was a very handsome one, and attracted a good deal of attention, but it was the two occupants Robyn noted. Gowned as exquisitely as ever, Lady Clyde was sitting up with the driver of the phaeton, gaily greeting everyone who passed. Sir Francis, tooling the ribbons as well as he contrived to do everything, appeared quite recovered from his ordeal and in high spirits too.

"Oh, there is Sir Francis and Lady Clyde," Mrs Fordingbridge cried when she too caught sight of the phaeton which had stopped and was immediately surrounded by people anxious to speak with the handsome couple. "How fortunate; you wished to have words with her."

Robyn pushed her hands further into her fur-lined muff. "Aunt Lizzie, as you can see, Sir Francis and Lady Clyde are already well-occupied and if we stop we shall only cause a crush."

When they passed, the disconcerted Mrs Fordingbridge nodded to the couple in the phaeton, but Robyn kept her eyes firmly on the way ahead although she was very much aware of her guardian's look which followed them.

As the carriage made its way towards the gate, Robyn discovered she was shaking, although she did not know why she should.

"They are a handsome couple, do you not agree?" Mrs Fordingbridge ventured, echoing, as it happened, Robyn's own thoughts.

"Yes," she agreed in a muted voice, staring down at her muff.

"Lord Clyde is also a charming man. The marchioness is a fortunate woman."

"I cannot help but feel desperately sorry for him. I only wonder he can still claim Sir Francis amongst his friends when all of London must know he has made him a cuckold."

Mrs Fordingbridge looked shocked. "My dear, you must not voice such thoughts."

Robyn smiled tightly. "One must know but not speak of such matters, it appears. I do not suppose Lord Clyde is the only man Sir Francis has cuckolded. There must be a veritable army of them."

"Robyn please! Enough of this talk. You are very naive if you think gentlemen should not have their diversions, and that includes Lord Clyde too. It is quite natural, you know."

The girl smiled again, but this time she looked at her relative. "Did Mr Fordingbridge have his diversions too?"

The woman's eyes opened wide. "Mr Fordingbridge was a country curate, and apart from a short Season in Town during which we met and married, he did not come up again."

Robyn smiled genuinely now, something which lit up her entire being and on occasions caused many a male heart to flutter.

"Dear Aunt Lizzie, I do believe you are a puritan at heart."

"And so are you, my dearest child, for all your outspokenness."

When they arrived back at Albemarle Street, Mrs Fordingbridge hurried up to her room whilst Robyn paused to peruse the calling cards and invitations which had arrived in their absence. As she lifted a posy of flowers to her face—brought by an admirer—she wondered for the first time what she would do if Sir Francis decided to accept one of the offers made for her. He could so easily grow weary of her and solve his problems in this tempting way. She could not think of one young man she might even begin to regard as a marriage partner even if she were so inclined to do. Certainly there was no one she could love, had she wished to, and more importantly none of them were weak enough to be disregarded after the ceremony. The notion, now it had entered her head, began to disturb her.

"Miss Wentworth!"

At the peremptory use of her name she dropped the posy and turned on her heel to come face to face with Sir Francis himself. Her eyes opened wide at the sight of him in the doorway. She and Mrs Fordingbridge had returned to Albemarle Street directly so, she realised, if Sir

Francis had arrived so soon after he must have made a special effort to do so.

He was still wearing his riding coat, the fit of which was immaculate. As so often was the case he wore no wig and his thick, dark hair was caught back in a ribbon. Unlike most men of her acquaintance he eschewed the use of paint and had never been seen to wear a patch. Ominously, it appeared to her at that moment, he still held his riding whip.

"Sir Francis," she said unsteadily and he continued to regard her with an unfriendly eye.

At last she could hold his gaze no longer and she lowered her eyes to his boots which showed not the slightest splash or blemish, but gleamed as if they were newly-blacked.

He stepped to one side to allow her to pass. "A few moments of your time if you please, Miss Wentworth."

With a feeling of great foreboding Robyn swept into the library. There seemed no doubt that his attitude was a hostile one which made her suspect she was in for a setdown and before he even spoke anger began to rise up inside her.

Walking away from her, he did not invite her to be seated and she steeled herself to receive whatever he might have to say with her customary spirit.

"Miss Wentworth," he said in a steady voice

147

as he threw the riding whip down on to the table, "what moves you to behave with such unspeakable incivility?"

She stepped back a pace and then, recovering her surprise, she tossed back her head and replied, "I . . . cannot conceive what you may mean."

He swung round on his heel to face her, clasping his hands behind his back. She felt as if she were being treated as an erring schoolgirl and that did nothing to calm her indignation.

"In plain view of a score of people acquainted with us all, you deliberately cut Lady Clyde this afternoon."

Robyn's eyes opened wide. "Cut her! I did no such thing. You were both engaged with several persons and I deemed it best not to stop and intrude."

"Did you indeed?" he asked in a low, menacing voice. "I find that a paltry excuse, and what is more it is a dishonest one."

She stiffened. "I shall pen a note to Lady Clyde immediately, begging her forgiveness, and all those petty enough to believe I would cut one who has befriended me will see that is not so on the very next occasion we are together in public."

He continued to gaze at her sombrely. "That might not be for some considerable time, Miss Wentworth."

Her gaze had become fixed on his diamond cravat pin, but now she looked at him uncomprehendingly. "What do you mean?"

"As the common courtesies of a social life in this town are so difficult for you to learn, I think it best if you cried off all invitations in the coming month to reflect on them the better."

She shook her head. "You cannot mean that."

"I most certainly do." He smiled faintly. "I would have thought you'd be pleased. By your own admission you dislike it all so heartily."

"But Lady Clyde's theatrical soiree . . . I am to play Desdemona . . ." Her lips twisted with irony. "Oh, you would not thwart Lady Clyde's plans, would you?"

He looked away, seemingly disinterested now. "I am persuaded she will find someone to replace you with very little difficulty."

As he picked up a document from the desk in a gesture of dismissal, she could contain her fury no longer. Unable to suppress a cry of anguish she hurled herself forward and her hand struck out towards his face. Quicker than she, he half turned and caught her wrist in a vice-like grip which caused her to wince, but it prevented her nails raking his cheeks.

His eyes blazed with fury and she could not maintain her own anger. "I did not deliberately cut Lady Clyde," she gasped.

"No, Miss Wentworth, you intended the snub for *me*, did you not?"

Her curls were now coming loose, hanging untidily about her cheeks which had grown very red. He kept hold of her wrist, drawing her unwillingly closer to him.

"Did you not, Miss Wentworth?" he insisted.

"*Yes.*" The admission was drawn out of her with agonising slowness.

"I do not stand in your way above the necessary, so why do you insist on this state of constant warfare?"

She still kept her face averted and he insisted, tugging at her wrist so she winced again. "Why, Robyn? Why do you deliberately seek to defy and anger me?"

"If you do not know," she answered in a small voice, "I cannot tell you."

He continued to stare at her furiously for a few moments before he thrust her away from him with some considerable force which caused her to stumble a little. "Be gone with you then. Out of my sight! And you need not be concerned for your social life. I shall not deprive the salons of your dazzling presence—this time!"

The moment she was released from his grip she went running across the library and when she reached the door she glanced back to where he stood. He had his back towards her, his head bent and his hands resting on the desk top.

With tears flowing down her cheeks she fled out of the library and up the stairs to her own room.

Ten

"Do you not think we should have rehearsed together for this evening?" Robyn asked of Lady Clyde as Ella helped her into her gown of oyster satin, the one the marchioness had deemed most fitting for Desdemona.

"There has not been the time, my dear. Besides, I have heard everyone speak their lines and I can assure you it will be perfect even though no one expects it to be. Nothing is more enjoyable than an unwitting error. It is only fun after all."

"I assure you it is more than that to me," Robyn told her as she sat down at the dressing table to be enveloped in a powdering robe.

Lady Clyde chuckled. "Neither is it to Clyde, my dear. There has scarce been a night when he has not come to my room, would you believe, to practise his lines? I am beginning to believe my charms are fading."

"I am sure you know they are not, Lady Clyde." She looked at the marchioness through the mirror. "There are many men who desire you."

"It is very gratifying, I own. I feel you will be similarly placed even after many years of marriage. No, no, Ella, leave the patches alone," she said as the maid reached out for the porcelain box. "Miss Wentworth must contrive to be as simply dressed as possible."

Looking at herself in the mirror, Robyn raised one eyebrow ironically, for her gown was decorated with a profusion of lace and ruffles, and her hair was piled high with curls both real and false, all of which had been smothered with powder.

Lady Clyde got to her feet, apparently satisfied with Robyn's appearance at last. "I must return home without delay and attend to matters there." She bent to kiss Robyn's cheek. "Until tonight, my dear. *Adieu*, and good luck."

Robyn smiled at her uncertainly, feeling at that moment both guilt and affection. She had not reckoned on becoming fond of Lady Clyde. It would have been much better if she could have remained hostile to everyone connected with Sir Francis Derringham.

However, such disquieting thoughts soon went

from her mind the moment she arrived at Clyde House after the carriage bearing both Mrs Fordingbridge and herself had taken its turn in the long line of conveyances waiting to discharge their passengers.

So many carriages emblazoned with aristocratic coats of arms, accompanied, as most of them were by running footmen holding aloft blazing torches, was sufficient to transform that part of Park Lane into a place of wonder. Lady Clyde was one of the foremost hostesses of the *ton* and invitations to every diversion devised by her were eagerly sought, so Robyn fully expected the mansion to be filled with people, and she was not disappointed.

All the public rooms were thronged with ladies in fine jewels and gowns, gentlemen both sombrely attired and those dandies in their exaggerated fashions. As she mingled with those people of her acquaintance Robyn realised for the first time that she had come to enjoy the social life far more than she would admit—even to herself.

After a while Lady Clyde herself came to seek her out. "I was told you had arrived, but what a crush! These soirees of mine are all the crack now. We shall soon begin, however and let us trust that all goes well, for our last soiree was most successful . . ."

Robyn looked at her with interest. "What was performed on that occasion?"

"We made out our adaptation of *The School for Scandal*. Of all things, I played Lady Teazle! Ah, the servants are directing everyone to the ballroom. It would be best if you waited in an anteroom from now on, so that you may compose yourself."

As she began to move away Robyn said, a mite uncomfortably, "Now that the evening has arrived I am sadly discomposed."

Lady Clyde gave her an encouraging smile. "Recall you are only amongst friends."

After a moment's hesitation Robyn asked, "Does Sir Francis intend to be here, for I have not seen him?"

Lady Clyde laughed and Robyn fluttered her fan, for her cheeks had grown uncomfortably hot. "Oh, indeed he is, but he is at present upstairs calming poor Frederick who always gets into a pucker at this stage in the proceedings."

Robyn made her way up the great staircase to the ballroom where curtains had been rigged up to simulate a stage. As Mrs Fordingbridge went to take her seat with the rest of the guests Robyn paced up and down the small anteroom, but her natural anxiety was almost totally eclipsed by her excitement. The marchioness had gone in search of the other players and at present a vapid miss by the name of Adeline Copsley was reciting some of the dullest verse Robyn had ever heard.

As she silently urged the others to hurry, so anxious was she to begin, she scarcely noticed the arrival of another. When she turned around at last the half smile of greeting on her face faded somewhat at the sight of her guardian—made-up as the Moor of Venice.

"Sir Francis?" she said uncertainly.

"Ah, so you recognise me? I wonder how many others will be so astute?"

"Where is Lord Clyde?"

"On his way, my dear. He is still trying to become the wicked Iago, but I fear he is too good-natured to succeed. He has not the manner, you see."

"Iago! But . . . I had no notion you would be playing the part of Othello. No one told me . . ."

He opened the door a little, peering out at the assembled audience. "I am always Lady Clyde's leading man," he confided, and she did not miss the heavy irony in his voice.

Inevitably she became angry then and disconcerted too, turning away from him to hide it. "I did note your interest in theatricals the evening we were at Drury Lane," she said with equal irony. "I trust that Mrs Wilcox is well."

"The last time I set eyes on her she was in excellent health. She will be gratified to hear of your concern."

Robyn scarce knew what to say next. Nothing dismayed him and he could so easily turn everything she said and did to his own advantage.

But that was the least which troubled her at that precise moment. She was aware of what would be expected of her as Desdemona, be it only an evening's diversion—and she could not bear the thought of having him as her leading man.

He closed the door quietly. "Be assured, Miss Wentworth, I did decline the honour initially, but it soon transpired that Lady Clyde could find no man willing to murder you with any degree of reality."

She gasped and turned to him again. "Your wit, if indeed it can be considered that, is entirely lost upon me, Sir Francis. Had I known ..." A malicious look suddenly came into her eye. "Do you truly believe you can play a cuckold with conviction?"

He waved one hand in the air. "Othello was not a cuckold. He was merely a victim of his own blind jealousy."

Vexedly, she snapped shut her fan. "Oh, I simply cannot pretend to be a faithful and loving wife if you are that man."

He smiled, not the least put out. "You do not have to. Recall, Othello was not convinced."

She stamped her foot. " 'Tis impossible. Can you not see that? Of all people to act great lovers we are the last two who should."

"I cannot conceive why not, my dear. It will last for no more than an hour and then you can go back to hating me," he answered with an infuriating complacency.

She made to go past him. "I shall go immediately and tell Lady Clyde I cannot go on."

He caught her arm as she made to go by him. The amusement in his eyes faded to be replaced by a look of steel. "Miss Wentworth, you will not cry off at this hour. I will not have Lady Clyde humiliated so in front of all her guests."

"So you humiliate me instead!" she challenged, choking back her tears.

"If you choose to call it that." He let go of her arm. "Come now. Save the drama for later. You fancy yourself as an actress; this is your opportunity to show your prowess. I am told invariably great stage partners hate each other heartily. Next time you shall be Lady Macbeth, which is more suiting your talents."

Old Lord Harmsby, who was to play Brabantio, arrived, struggling to straighten his wig, and his presence precluded any further badinage. Robyn moved away from her guardian just as the marchioness came in, accompanied by her husband, who was clutching the manuscript of the play, several others who were playing small parts, and Lady Sherley who had agreed to take the part of Emilia.

"Now dearest, do not get into a pucker," Lady

Clyde was saying to her husband. "You will do very well, I am sure." She turned to the others in obvious delight. "I have the honour of imparting a piece of splendid news to you all." Sir Francis gave Robyn one last look before returning his more bland attention to the marchioness. "His Royal Highness, the Prince of Wales has honoured us with his gracious presence tonight."

Robyn, who had been contemplating the awful prospect of being held close to that dreadful man, now had her thoughts diverted. "What!" she cried. "You cannot mean it."

"He has just now taken his seat."

Still not quite believing it, Robyn went to open the door a crack and sure enough the handsome young heir to the throne was seated with his retinue at the front of the audience.

"Lady Clyde, what shall I do?"

"Do as you always intended to do, naturally dear," she answered.

Robyn continued to appear agitated and her guardian told her, "Never fear, he will not order your execution if you do not please him." The others laughed to the girl's further mortification. "Robyn," he went on in a gentle voice, "recall I shall be out there with you."

This reminder hardly served to reassure her. In fact this evening, which she had looked forward to so eagerly, was fast turning into a nightmare.

"Perchance Miss Wentworth does not wish to continue," Lady Sherley suggested, her eyes alight with malice.

"Tush!" Lady Clyde retorted. "I shall acept no such thing," and then she went out, beaming at them all, ready to announce the commencement of the play.

Robyn eyed Sir Francis coldly as he went out of the room accompanied by the others except for Lady Sherley. The moment he had gone she was assailed by panic and even contemplated flight until she noted that the other lady was still eyeing her spitefully.

"You must be delighted at the honour of being asked to play the lead when you have had no experience of theatricals before."

"If you deem it such an honour, Lady Sherley, I would gladly exchange places with you."

The woman laughed without mirth. "Oh no dear, that would not do. I have not the . . . er . . . connection with Lady Clyde."

Robyn did nothing more than cast her a withering look before she sank down into a chair to await her summons to the floor. Darkly she anticipated what should have been a pleasurable evening with dread, and as usual it was all due to the fault of Sir Francis Derringham.

* * *

Applause echoed in Robyn's ears as she faced Lady Clyde's guests after the final drama had been enacted. The play had been received well by those eager for new diversions, she realised, although she was numb to all but her bruised feelings. Not once had he spared them. As Othello, Sir Francis seemed to have delighted in holding her close whenever the action allowed it.

Out of the corner of her eye Robyn noticed that the Prince of Wales was actually on his feet.

"His Highness wishes to meet you," Lady Clyde told her before she could escape, and together with her guardian and the marchioness she was obliged to approach him, still seething because of the many deviations Sir Francis had made from Shakespeare's lines, much to the amusement of the guests.

As Sir Francis chatted unselfconsciously with the future King, Robyn, still feeling ill-used, noted that he was not dressed in the height of fashion, but he did wear the Order of the Garter and was very handsome.

At last he did turn his attention to her and she sank into a deep curtsey. "You did very well, Miss Wentworth," he told her. "My handkerchief is damp with tears."

"I am deeply honoured, sir."

"I am given to understand that you are the ward of Sir Francis."

Robyn could not help but draw in a sharp breath. "That is so, sir."

"He is a lucky man, and deservedly so. If it were not for Sir Francis I would be King today and I find life as the Prince of Wales too rewarding not to be aware of it." He laughed before adding, "It has been a pleasure meeting you, Miss Wentworth, and I do hope it will not be long before we find ourselves in company again."

Just before she sank into a curtsey again Robyn raised her eyes to his at last and was taken aback to see the admiration in them. She felt quite numb and was hardly aware that the Prince was being escorted away by Lord and Lady Clyde.

"That was not so bad, was it?" her guardian asked, causing her to start nervously. "He was very taken by you."

She twisted her hands together in anguish. "Everything is far worse than anything I ever imagined!" she cried and turned on her heel, fleeing to the anteroom whilst Sir Francis went to remove the blacking from his face, and the other participants to rejoin their friends. To her own disgust the moment Robyn reached the anteroom she collapsed onto a chaise longue and burst into a torrent of noisy tears, the reason for which even she could not understand.

It was in this condition that Mrs Fordingbridge discovered her some time later. "Oh, my dear child, what is amiss? You did so well. Everyone is saying so, and the Prince! His Highness was enchanted by you."

She fumbled in her reticule for a vinaigrette which she held up to Robyn's face. Robyn was just in the act of pushing it away when Lady Clyde arrived.

"Oh, so this is where you are hiding . . . Oh, dear, not an attack of the vapours, I trust."

"I am not vapourish."

"I can vouch for that," agreed Mrs Fordingbridge.

The marchioness smiled sympathetically. "I perfectly understand, my dear. It is merely that your sensibilities are overset. More than half the guests are similarly afflicted. Only just now I have left Sir Humphrey Creighton with tears running down his cheeks. And how his rouge has run!"

She bent down to pat Robyn's hand as the girl attempted to dry her cheeks. "You were the triumph, you know. Everyone says so. They adore you. The Prince too! Only think of it, Robyn. You might yet oust Mrs Robinson in his affections. You could even become the Princess of Wales!"

Robyn cast her a look of disgust. "Everyone

knows the Prince will marry a German princess."

"Prince George is remarkably self-willed. I am persuaded he will marry a woman of his own choice, but that is of no account. You did so well, my dear."

"Considering Sir Francis insisted on making us all look foolish."

"Oh, I cannot own to that, my dear, although it was only in fun. I have never seen Ophelia played with such spirit, but I do not believe the play lost anything by your interpretation of the role. You must act for us again, and very soon!"

Robyn straightened up then. "Oh no, Lady Clyde. I could not. Once is quite enough."

"I dare say we can discuss the matter at length another time. For now I must leave you to Mrs Fordingbridge's ministrations; supper is about to be served and I must go to my guests, but do join us as soon as you can, dear. Everyone is so anxious to congratulate you."

When she had gone Mrs Fordingbridge looked to her charge anxiously. "Are you feeling better, Robyn?"

"Yes, Aunt Lizzie, much," she answered, drawing a deep sigh.

"Do you still wish to take up acting on the stage?"

Robyn laughed mirthlessly. "No. I do not think such a career would suit me after all."

The woman looked pleased. "I am so gratified to hear it, Robyn. I do not think it would be at all the thing. You are all done-up over this and I did so fear your head would be turned to-night."

"Put your fears to rest, Aunt Lizzie." She laid her head back on the cushions of the chaise longe. "Sometimes I believe I was born under a three-halfpenny planet."

"That is arrant nonsense. You have led an exceeding lucky life. When has anything teased you?"

Robyn had no opportunity to answer, for a noise in the doorway caused her to look up to see Sir Francis standing there, looking at her. She immediately stiffened, for she could never relax in his presence. He had changed his clothes and once more looked the fashionable and urbane gentleman, rather than the demented Moor he had portrayed so well.

"Mrs Fordingbridge," he said without taking his eyes off Robyn, "would you be so good as to leave us a few minutes? You may leave the door open if you wish."

Before Robyn could beg her to refuse the request, Mrs Fordingbridge did as she was bid. "Perhaps you would bring Robyn into supper when you have finished your coze. She is feeling much recovered now."

Robyn was very much aware of him as he

came further into the room, still fixing her with his steady gaze. She averted her eyes, only recalling too vividly his close embrace in the final moments of the act, something she could hardly bear to reflect upon. In retrospect that had been the true reason for her uncharacteristic attack of the vapours.

"How are you feeling now?" he enquired politely.

"I am perfectly all right."

"Lady Clyde told me you were overcome."

"Everyone is making too much of it."

"Robyn," he said a moment later, in a gentle voice which he had never used to her before, "what is grieving you?"

"Nothing," she answered sharply. "It has all been too much for me, that is all."

He sat down on the edge of the chaise longue, much to her alarm, taking her hand in his. Initially she attempted to withdraw it but his grip was too strong and she looked at him fearfully.

"It would have to be a stupid man who could not perceive that you are deeply unhappy and have been since your arrival in Town. It is time you and I spoke frankly about your grievances." He considered her hand with undue interest. "If I have done something which angers you, then speak of it now."

"You are mistaken. There is nothing, and we must go into supper."

He let her hand go and thankfully she swung her legs to the floor, but before she could stand up his hands gripped her shoulders, causing her to stiffen against them.

"Now you have tasted life in Society you can if you wish return to the country. I can arrange it for you. Is that what you really want?"

"No. It makes no odds where I reside," she answered in a whisper.

There was a further silence before he said, "Robyn, if I am guilty of some wrong, you must tell me. There is no calumny which cannot be put right."

His soft voice was close to her ear, his breath cool on her neck. Momentarily she closed her eyes in an attempt to stop the tears squeezing beneath her lids, but as he began to pull her closer to him she jerked away, springing to her feet. He looked startled, which was not surprising, and as he got to his feet too she gathered up her skirts and fled the room leaving him calling her name.

He was still in the anteroom when Lady Clyde found him some time later. He was staring blindly into space and she immediately looked concerned.

"Francis, where is Miss Wentworth?"

Sighing, he answered, "I do not know. I tried to speak with her but as usual it was impossible. I am at a loss what to do next."

She held his arm. "Poor, poor Francis. These past few months have not been easy for you. You dreaded taking on this guardianship but everything is far worse than you feared." When he made no answer she went on, "I hate to see you so despondent. Is there nothing I can do?"

He looked at her at last, smiling fondly. "You have done more than enough."

"It is not exasperation you feel now, is it, my dear? You are experiencing something quite different. How ironic that is after all these years of immunity. There are those who would say you are deserving of this fate. And stubborn pride ensures that you will not pursue her."

He looked down at her. "You have always known me so well, Virginia."

She stood on tip-toe and, putting her arms around him, kissed him, whereupon he enfolded her in his arms and pressed his lips to her cheek.

Eleven

Robyn fled headlong towards the company of others, heedless that the tears on her cheeks would cause the very comment she wished to avoid. A group of guests were coming towards her and she slowed her pace before dodging behind a marble pillar until they had gone. She drew a sigh and leaned back against the coolness of the marble, realising that whilst she did not want to be alone, neither did she have any desire for company after all, although she would be obliged to pretend she was happy for the remainder of the evening. But what, she asked herself, about the rest of my life?

She was about to continue on her way to the supper room when she paused again, wringing her hands together in anguish. Suddenly she turned and hurried back towards the anteroom where she had left her guardian. Guardian. How that title mocked her. She closed her eyes once more, experiencing excruciating anguish as she recalled the feel of his arms around her. It was just too much to bear.

All at once, though, she was no more the uncertain child she had been for so long. She would, after all, speak with him, for she could no longer shoulder alone the burden she had carried with her for so long. He too must share it, although her heart ached at the very thought.

As she approached the room she became hesitant again. So much bitterness had been stored inside her she was afraid of the consequences of setting it free at last. Besides, all that bitterness had been a comfort to her, a protection, in fact. But no longer. One thing this evening had shown her was the depth of her own vulnerability.

The door was still half open just as she had left it as she put her hand on the knob. As she did so she recognised Lady Clyde's voice from within. Robyn froze but then, when she dared to look, she saw the marchioness and Sir Francis locked in a tight and loving embrace.

She drew back as if burned, clapping one hand to her lips to stifle a cry. Once again she turned on her heel, fleeing that room as if it were infected with the plague. Tears squeezed from her eyes despite all her efforts to force them back, and she could not credit her own distress at being faced with the proof of what she had always known.

And yet a treacherous voice within her own heart told her the answer, and it was one almost too painful to bear. Of all men, why Sir Francis? she asked herself.

The noise and laughter emanating from the supper room drifted through the first floor of the house, checking her flight as she approached. She could face no one. No one at all.

A hand touching the sleeve of her gown caused her to gasp and turn in alarm to find Captain Blackwell looking at her with concern. "Miss Wentworth, I have been seeking you everywhere. I do not think I need to add my own admiration to that of everyone else, but I beg you to allow me the honour of escorting you into supper."

Brushing a tear from her cheek, she answered breathlessly, "I thank you, Captain Blackwell, but I am not in the least hungry and it is cooler here."

"I believe I understand your need for quiet, Miss Wentworth, but you will be entirely of a different mind when the gaming tables are set up after supper."

She gave him an absent glance without truly looking at him. "You must know that gaming is forbidden to me now."

He smiled deprecatingly. "I had not thought you so biddable. Sir Francis is bound to honour your debts whatever else he might say."

She looked at him directly for the first time. "If I dare incur any, Sir Francis will declare my wagers void at every house I attend. You can appreciate that I am anxious to avoid such a humiliation in front of my friends."

"That is altogether too harsh. I cannot conceive he would be so hard-hearted."

Robyn was obliged to smile then. "I do not think we need doubt his word on it, Captain Blackwell."

"Your guardian is a hard man to decry such harmless pastimes, especially as he indulges his own fancy in that direction."

To Robyn now the entire issue of her gaming was totally irrelevant and she was beginning to be irritated at the direction of the conversation.

"It is wrong of us to discuss it. Pray excuse me, Captain Blackwell, I think I shall go into supper after all." As she turned to go she swayed on her feet and he steadied her.

"Ma'am, you appear to be in some distress."

Immediately she averted her eyes, " 'Tis nothing."

"A man cannot be as devoted as I and not note every mood of one's beloved. Can I be of any assistance?"

"No, Captain Blackwell. There is no help to be had. I am in torment, a hell not of my making."

He looked shocked at so blunt a statement.

"Ma'am, I am indeed moved at such an admission. How may I serve you?"

"You cannot," she answered breathlessly. "Life for me is impossible."

"If you honour me with your confidence you may rely upon my discretion."

She laughed mirthlessly. "It is a secret that must go with me to the grave. Sufficient to say I am in an intolerable situation and at a total loss how to escape it."

He regarded her for a moment or two before saying, "I suspect I know who, at least, is the cause of all your grief, Miss Wentworth."

She smiled faintly. "You do not know the whole of it, Captain Blackwell, but your concern is most warming. I know I was rash in speaking, but as you observed I am in dire distress and needed a sympathethic confidante."

"I hope I shall always be that, ma'am." He hesitated a moment before saying, "You are already fully aware of my feelings for you, but if I offered now to take you away from your torment and make you my wife, I fear we shall only be storing up further grief. Your guardian would retain control of your fortune and we shall be obliged to live in penury."

"I am touched by your concern, sir. Believe me, if it were only possible for you to be of help to me I would avail myself of your services."

Just at that moment Lady Clyde and Sir

Francis came strolling arm in arm down the corridor on their way to the supper room. Robyn stared at them furiously as they passed, Lady Clyde nodding and Sir Francis merely frowning with disapproval.

As soon as they had gone Robyn turned to Captain Blackwell once more. "Would you truly do anything to help me?"

"You may rely on it, ma'am."

She drew in a sharp breath. "Very well. To be plain, I cannot bear to remain in London a day longer. I must go away. But there is no place for me to go. Can you help me?"

He laughed uncertainly. "Miss Wentworth, everything I possess is yours, but that is very little and money is needed for such a scheme."

"I have my mother's jewels, although they are only modest in comparison . . ."

" 'Tis better than nothing, but will not Sir Francis come in pursuit of you?"

"No doubt," she answered grimly, "but I have been nought but a trial to him and he will not make too much of a business of it. Besides," she went on in a voice suddenly hard, "I have decided it necessary for me to leave the country and I do not intend ever to return."

He smiled. "I am persuaded you will change your mind when the time arrives for you to claim your inheritance." She said nothing and a moment later he went on, "Miss Wentworth, are you quite certain this is the course you wish to take?"

She turned away. "Forgive me, Captain Blackwell, it was a foolish thought and I am presuming too much on your affections. It was a cork-brained scheme and will not do. Pray forget all I have said."

"How can I forget your distress, Miss Wentworth?" As her eyes remained averted she was not aware of the triumphant smile on his face. He was only too well aware that he now possessed a weapon with which he could strike a blow at Sir Francis as well as take himself an heiress for a bride. "I have a plan," he said in a mild tone of voice which caused her to look at him with interest. "It would suit us both. If we go about this in the proper way we can be in France before Sir Francis is aware of your absence."

"*We*, Captain Blackwell?"

"I could not possibly allow you to travel alone." His eyes took on a hard look. "There is nothing here for me with you gone, and I beg you to recall if you marry me you will be for ever free of him."

She wrung her hands together. "Yes," she breathed. "Yes, indeed I will. Very well," she answered. "You and I deal well together and you have been a loyal friend. I shall not deny you your heart's desire. Once we are in France I shall marry you."

He looked triumphant but Robyn could derive no pleasure from her decision. "I have a plan," he said, "which will set us up for our new life."

"You must tell me all about it," she answered in a dull voice.

"There is no time. If you are insistent upon going . . ."

"I *must*," she said fervently.

"Then trust me."

She looked uncertain for a moment or two and then a steely look came into her eye and she held her head erect.

"Captain Blackwell, what would you have me do?"

Mrs Fordingbridge came hurrying down the stairs and having reached the hall ran first one way and then the other.

"Where is Sir Francis?" she asked in obvious distress. "I must speak to Sir Francis."

"He is in the library, madam," answered one of the footmen, "but he is engaged with his secretary on matters of business."

"Then pray tell him I must have words with him."

"Sir Francis does not wish to be disturbed, madam."

"Don't stand there bandying words with

me, man," she cried, for once asserting her authority. "Tell him I am here immediately."

Before he could do so she brushed past him, thrusting the library door open herself. Both Sir Francis and the young man he employed as secretary looked up in alarm. The baronet immediately got to his feet.

"Mrs Fordingbridge, what is the meaning of this intrusion?"

"I beg your pardon, Sir Francis, but it is Robyn . . ."

A look of irritation crossed his face. "What has she done now, ma'am?"

The woman advanced into the room, brandishing a piece of paper. "She was absconded!"

For a moment he looked disbelieving and then said, "You must be mistaken."

"She is gone and I have her note!"

He digested this information for a moment or two before turning to his secretary. "That will be all for now, Carter."

The young man made a bow and left the room, although he looked as though he would rather stay.

"Now, ma'am, what is this nonsense?" Sir Francis asked, coming from behind the desk.

"See for yourself," she answered, thrusting the paper in front of him. "This was on her pillow when Ella went to take her some breakfast chocolate this morning. She must have gone last night immediately after returning from Lady Clyde's."

He took the note from her, reading it quickly and then crushing it in his fist. "What is this 'awesome burden' she can no longer bear?"

"I have no notion, Sir Francis, although I have oft tried to ascertain what is grieving her. She has been possessed of some wildness ever since Colonel Wentworth died."

He waved his hand in the air. "That is of no moment now. Had you no notion that she was planning to abscond?"

"None at all, Sir Francis. Robyn has always kept her own counsel, even when she was a child, but of late she has been in good spirits, I fancy.

"What is that she has written as a postcript, Sir Francis? I cannot quite understand."

He glanced at the note again after smoothing it out. "*My only love sprung from my only hate,*" he read out loud.

"What can that mean?"

He smiled faintly. "It is a line from *Romeo and Juliet.*"

"Oh, Robyn and her playacting," she said irritably. "What is that *now*?"

"More to the point, ma'am, where can she have gone?" he murmured, almost to himself.

"I think she may have eloped. You must send to Gretna to stop it."

He looked at her sharply. "Why do you say so? Have you proof?"

"No, but there can be no other alternative."

"I cannot agree." He frowned, staring into space. "But she must have had help." He looked at the woman again. "Has she taken a maid with her?"

"No. Poor Ella is beside herself. We did look in the press and it appears Robyn had taken only a few necessary items with her. Sir Francis, what are we to do?"

"Naturally, bring her back."

"But there will be the most dreadful scandal."

"Not if we do not get into a pucker over this, but even so that is the least of our concerns."

"I feel I have failed her most dreadfully."

He stared into space once again. "No more than I, ma'am."

"Oh, if some harm has befallen her, I shall never forgive myself."

He smiled faintly as she moved across the room. "Calm yourself, dear lady, all is not lost. Firstly I shall ascertain if Captain Blackwell is still at his lodgings, for I feel he is involved in this matter. The last time I clapped eyes on her she was in deep conversation with that scoundrel."

"Elopement with Captain Blackwell," Mrs Fordingbridge said in a shocked whisper.

He gave a sharp order to the footman outside the door before returning to the room. "If that transpires I vow he shall not live to enjoy the fruits of the union. However, I had heard a rumour that he was about to flee the country to escape the duns. If he has indeed gone he might have persuaded Robyn to go with him. That is the direction I must take.

"Now, ma'am, you must excuse me. I shall prepare to ride to Dover as soon as I have news of Blackwell."

As she went towards the door Mrs Fordingbridge paused to look at him. "You are fonder of the chit than you will admit."

He smiled faintly. "You are very astute, ma'am. Only Robyn herself seems unaware of it."

She seemed about to say something more but then hurried from the room, aware that she would be in a fidge until she had news of the girl.

Twelve

Only the hooting of an owl and the steady clip-clop of hooves broke the stillness of the night. Trees which lined the road loomed menacingly all around them and Robyn shivered as she pulled her cloak around her.

Riding slightly ahead of her Captain Blackwell said, "Is anything amiss?"

"Why can we not put up in an inn, Captain Blackwell?"

"When we reach Dover you may rest and eat your fill, my dear, but until we are safely there we must make haste. Indeed, I shall not rest easy until we are at the other side of the Channel."

The knowledge that she would not see the shores of England for at least eight years smote her heart. There was no joy in going forward, but certainly no possibility of going back.

"It is fortunate there is a moon and a clear sky so we can travel by night," her companion observed.

"We have been riding for an unconscionable time," she answered wearily.

"We must make as much speed as we can before either of us is missed. You would not have Sir Francis overtake us, would you?"

"He can have no notion we are on this road, or even that I am with you."

He chuckled softly as if the notion pleased him. "Do not underestimate Sir Francis, my dear. He is an astute man, although I am persuaded you are correct on this occasion."

She peered into the gloom at the man on horseback close by her. "Why do you hate him so?"

"He denied me your hand in marriage."

"That was as much my decision as his, Captain Blackwell. I feel that your hatred of him is of a different origin."

"We shall be companions in this great adventure so I may as well admit I hate all men such as he; full of consequence, and privileged, unaware and uncaring of the daily struggle merely to keep ahead of the duns. Men such as he find it easy to condemn a lack or morality whereas their own morals are equally weak. Do you wonder I harbour such hatred in my heart?"

She could not answer and as they came to a

bend in the road and a thicket he reined in his horse, saying, "Would you wish to rest a few minutes, Miss Wentworth?"

"Yes, I thank you."

He lifted her down from the horse and even when her feet touched the ground he did not release her immediately. "My dear Miss Wentworth . . ." he said softly.

She pulled away from him. "When we are in France and married, Captain Blackwell."

A spasm of anger crossed his face. "Are you so unwilling to receive the embraces of your guardian, my dear?"

Robyn gasped. "What did you say?"

He smiled tightly in the darkness. "I was, you recall, present at Lady Clyde's last night. I saw the way he embraced you."

"It was merely a play!" she protested, glad that the darkness hid her blushes.

"Do not think to gammon me, my dear. I am wise to the ways of a woman's heart. When you begged to escape something intolerable, in a chit of your years there can be only one thing. Do you really think I was so stupid I could not know of it?"

She turned away. "We must never talk of it again. *Never!*"

"It shall be as you wish, my dear," he answered urbanely. "I am convinced you will come to appreciate my worth before too long a time has passed, and in the meantime I shall be obliged to hide my impatience."

"I am indebted to you for your help," she said uncertainly.

She went to sit on a tree stump. The moon was on the wane and the sky growing lighter. At Albemarle Street the servants would already be stirring, ready to meet the new day. She wondered how Sir Francis would react to her disappearance; with anger no doubt. Well she would not anger him again now.

"You are not sorry you have come?" he asked, breaking into her thoughts. "There is yet time for you to return, if that is what you wish."

"*No*," she answered, her eyes growing wide. "There is no going back." When he continued to look at her speculatively she said, "I cannot help but feel sorry for Mrs Fordingbridge. When she reads my note . . ."

He gripped her arm. "You say you left a note?"

"Oh, it contained no clue as to my direction, of that you may be assured, Captain Blackwell, but I am exceeding fond of my relative and I would not have her worry beyond what is absolutely necessary. And now, I pray you, unhand my arm."

He did so just as the sound of thunder became audible to them both. Anxious, and always aware of the possibility of pursuit, Robyn got to her feet, looking at him as a slow smile spread across his face.

"What is that?" she asked.

"It is the London Coach, of course. On time too, Miss Wentworth, and it could not suit us better." She continued to watch him as he went back to his horse and then she gasped when she saw him draw a pistol from the folds of his greatcoat.

"Captain Blackwell, what is this about?" she asked, rushing up to him. "Why do you have a pistol? Are we about to be set upon?"

He laughed in a way she had never witnessed in him before, nor in a way she much liked. "Quite the reverse, my dear. *We* are about to set ourselves up for our journey to France. We shall wish, quite naturally, to travel in style, and the coach is rich pickings indeed."

As the pounding of hooves grew louder, Robyn recoiled, horrified, watching in disbelief as he wound a muffler around the lower part of his face.

"You cannot mean to hold up a stage coach," she gasped.

"It will take but a few minutes of our time, and then we can be on our way again. Even at the gaming tables, you must own, money does not change hands so quickly or with such ease."

"But you intend to commit a crime; highway robbery."

"We need the blunt." He glanced at her. "You need not be in a fidge, my dear, for this is not my first escapade plying the high toby. You alone are privileged to know the identity of Captain Swell and to see him in action."

"You!" she gasped, her eyes wide with horror. "Captain Swell!"

"At your service, my dear," he answered, giving a slight bow. "Does this not suit your taste for adventure then?" At the sight of her horror-stricken expression he merely laughed. "If you wish you may assist me."

"No!"

He laughed softly. "I am not alone in my . . . trade, my dear. There is a veritable army of gentlemen who often find their pockets to let."

"It was you who held up Sir Francis and tried to kill him!" she cried, dashing forward as he swung into the saddle. Her face contorted with fury at the realisation.

"How astute of you, my dear. If I had succeeded neither of us would have cause to be here now." His voice suddenly grew hard. "No, remain concealed in this thicket and be ready to take flight when I call."

"I would not go with you for anything now!" she cried, railing him with her fists.

His horse reared slightly and he struggled to retain control of it, causing Robyn to stagger backwards.

"As you wish, my dear, but you sorely disappoint me. I had not taken you for a vapourish female, and we could have made our fortune on the roads of France. Think on it whilst you watch me at work."

He dug in his spurs and charged forward, pistol at the ready. Robyn hesitated only moments before she rushed towards her own mount. The sound of pounding hooves filled her head as she charged forward after Captain Blackwell, a cry of warning on her lips.

Suddenly there came a squealing of brakes, hastily applied. A woman screamed and a ball was discharged into the air, causing Robyn's horse to rear. As she struggled to retain control of her mount another shot was fired, making the horse rise again. This time she could not hold on. The world turned upside-down as she fell heavily to the ground, the breath momentarily knocked out of her body.

When she opened her eyes again, they were dazzled by the light of a lantern held over her, but she could, quite plainly hear a voice saying, "Look what we 'ave 'ere, a female tobyman!"

Sir Francis stripped off his gloves wearily and handed them to a footman before shrugging out of his sodden greatcoat. He was pale and unshaven, and there was an unusually gaunt look about his face.

189

Mrs Fordingbridge, waiting anxiously for his return, came hurrying down the stairs before he was halfway across the hall. "Sir Francis, have you any news of Robyn?"

As he raised his eyes to hers she knew the answer and she drew back, her eyes filling with tears. "What can have become of her?"

"She is not with Blackwell, that much I have ascertained." She looked at him hopefully and he went on, "That scoundrel has most certainly fled the country as I suspected. I enquired of them at Dover and it seems Blackwell was there the day before yesterday. He had breakfast at the *Crown and Anchor* but everyone I questioned, including the inn-keeper who provided him with breakfast, is insistent that he was entirely alone both before and when he boarded the packet boat."

"Then your gamble is lost, Sir Francis. She must have eloped with someone else."

"Have you had word of it?" he asked with sudden hopefulness.

Her head dropped. "No. Nothing since you left."

A sigh escaped him. "Then I would think not. You see, to elope, ma'am, Robyn would need a partner and if that were the case an irate parent would have been round here within the hour.

"Do you think she might have returned to her former home?"

Mrs Fordingbridge considered for a moment before answering. "I think not, Sir Francis. She has no sentimental attachment to it and if her object was to escape you . . ." She flushed before continuing, "Robyn would expect you to seek her out there."

"Quite so, but nevertheless I must send a messenger to make enquiries in that neighbourhood. She might have made the acquaintance of someone there of whom you know nothing. We cannot afford to ignore any avenue of investigation now."

"You have done more than enough, Sir Francis. There is nothing more you can do."

"There is one more thing," he answered thoughtfully. "As I said, I doubt if elopement is the answer, but nonetheless there is always the faint possibility that the man purporting to be Captain Blackwell in Dover just might not be he. As soon as I am rested I shall set out for Gretna."

Mrs Fordingbridge bit her lip. "Lady Clyde called after you had gone." When he looked at her curiously she went on, "Oh, she had merely called to bring Robyn a bottle of Eau de Chypre which had arrived that morning from Monsieur Houbigant's establishment in Paris, but she immediately discerned something was amiss and I was obliged to tell her . . ."

Sir Francis put a comforting hand on the woman's trembling arm. "You were quite right to do so."

"She has agreed to spread the story that Robyn has gone to spend a few days with a relative in the country, and I am to keep her informed of any news."

"That is good of her. No doubt she will also keep an ear open for any particle of news. Now, ma'am, you could do me a kindness . . ."

"Anything, Sir Francis, only name it."

"Order a cold collation to be brought to my room. That will save time, I fancy. I must leave as soon as is possible."

As she hurried away to do his bidding Sir Francis drew a sigh and went wearily up the stairs, anxious to make up for two nights of lost sleep in the space of a few hours.

"Gone more than a sen'night and no trace of her!" Sir Francis exclaimed, thumping his fist on the table in frustration.

Mrs Fordingbridge, seated before the table, began to weep. Her eyes were already red-rimmed from bouts of weeping, as were his although in his case it was due to lack of sleep.

"Ma'am, do not be so distressed," he said in a more gentle voice.

"It would appear she has disappeared from the face of the earth," she wailed.

"Be assured, if she is still in England she will be found. I have men still engaged in enquiring at the Channel ports, and I have myself made sure she did not go to Gretna. Now a Runner is employed exclusively on my behalf, checking with the families of those school friends whose names you noted."

"She did stay with friends when she was not at school. It was something Colonel Wentworth encouraged rather than have her come home, but as most of the girls are still at school themselves I cannot see how she can avail herself of their help."

He shook his head. "I confess, ma'am, I am at a loss as to what I can do next."

Mrs Fordingbridge dried her eyes. "Sir Francis, you have done everything possible. Why, I doubt if you have slept one night in a proper bed since Robyn disappeared. You look all done-up and you must needs rest . . ."

Once more his fist came slamming down on the table, "Dammit! I cannot rest until I know she is safe!"

The woman looked fearful. "Safe! There is one thing which heartens me, Sir Francis, and that is the fact that Robyn is quite able to look after herself."

"She is as vulnerable as any female, more so

perhaps for all her independent stance. She could so easily be prey to the machinations of evil people." When she shuddered he went on, "I am sorry if I have alarmed you more."

"You cannot," she admitted. "I am already beside myself. I am fully aware this country we live in is no place for a female on her own. Indeed, I have often attempted to tell her so when she was so set against taking a husband. Moreover, Robyn has no money save what she might raise on the sale of her jewels."

"That will be little enough," he said grimly, "without the necessary contacts."

During the heavy silence which descended upon them there came a knock at the front door. When a footman came in Sir Francis said immediately, "I cannot receive anyone."

"It is Lady Clyde, Sir Francis, and she begs to say her call is of the utmost urgency."

"By all means show her in," he answered then, hurrying towards the door himself.

The marchioness was obviously greatly disturbed, for as Mrs Fordingbridge got to her feet, Lady Clyde scarce glanced at her and Sir Francis was quick to note that his cousin's hat was not at quite the modish angle as was usual.

"Francis!" she cried the moment she was shown into the room. "I have news of Robyn at last."

Mrs. Fordingbridge gasped and Sir Francis clung to his cousin's trembling hands.

"Tell me all you know!"

"Oh, I can scarce believe it. 'Tis incredible, Francis. I am all of a tremble as you can see. Do you know Lord Purcell?"

"That old suckbottle."

She nodded. "He tipped the turn-key to see the prisoners at Newgate with some of his cronies, as is his wont, and he came immediately afterwards to see me, for he could scarce believe it too. Francis, Robyn is *there*—in Newgate!"

Her eyes opened wide with horror as Sir Francis let her hands go, stepping back. "Was he in his cups?"

"No. I vow he was quite sober. That is why I am in such a pucker."

Sir Francis was aghast. "He must be mistaken."

"Oh, I pray that he is, for she is convicted of highway robbery and is in the condemned cell!"

Mrs Fordingbridge cried out in anguish which attracted Lady Clyde's attention at last. "Francis!" she cried, pointing to the woman.

He leaped forward to catch the swooning woman before she could fall. He eased her onto a sofa whereupon Lady Clyde brought out her vinaigrette.

"Leave her to me, Francis. Only go now and see if Lord Purcell was correct."

He hesitated not a moment longer, rushing from the room and calling for his curricle to be brought round as the marchioness ministered to the insensible woman.

Sir Francis raised his cologne-soaked handkerchief to his face in an attempt to counter the fearful stench which met him as he followed the turn-key up the stairs.

"Why was no one informed when she was taken?" the baronet demanded. "Did she not request a lawyer to stand up for her?"

"As I understand it, yer worship, the chit wanted no one and would not even tell her name. Admitted the crime, she did, right before the beak."

Sir Francis pulled his greatcoat closer around him to ward off the dank chill which assaulted him, but he could not suppress a shiver. From somewhere nearby a soul howled in torment and another answered with an ear-piercing laugh.

He could not believe Robyn was in this place, condemned from her own mouth too. It was all a ghastly mistake, understandable too; Lord Purcell was invariably foxed at any time of the day. He had probably mistaken some unspeakable doxy for Robyn and the baronet resolved to seek him out at the earliest possible moment to demand an apology for it.

They came to the cell, occupied by felons both male and female. They had in common an appointment with the Tyburn hangman. The key grated in the lock and a young man dressed only in shirt and breeches came rushing over to the bars, startling Sir Francis who had been scanning the cell for sight of the creature Lord Purcell had mistaken for Robyn.

"They sent you to free me at last!" the man cried.

Sir Francis glanced at him absently, irritated by the distraction. "I regret not," and the young man's countenance contorted with pain whereupon he laid his head against the bars and howled with anguish.

"There she be," the turn-key told him.

He looked towards the corner to see someone huddled on filthy straw and suppressed the urge to vomit, so strong was the stench.

"Don't you ever clean out these cells?" he asked.

"No call for me to do so," the man replied. As Sir Francis went slowly into the cell, the turn-key warned, "Watch your purse, yer worship. They'll 'ave it off yer."

Sir Francis did not heed him; he went towards the corner of the cell, only to be stopped by a woman with hair like straw and whose gown was filthy and torn.

"You'll get nothin' from that one, so why don't you take me instead?"

Angrily he pushed her aside to be rewarded by a flow of invective which would normally have made him flinch, coming from a woman. The person huddled in the corner attracted his attention too much for him to bother about anything else just then. Whoever it was was dressed in breeches and jerkin, and he hesitated when he came closer. The light was poor, but sufficient for him to see that this poor, thin creature could not be Robyn Wentworth.

"Robyn?" he said softly nevertheless, feeling he should never have come on this fool's errand. Ever since his fruitless journey to Gretna he had become convinced that, somehow, despite all his enquiries Robyn *had* gone to the continent with Franklyn Blackwell.

A low chuckle from nearby caused him to look round sharply. An old, toothless crone who was squatting on the damp floor nearby, said, "That ain't no boy, sirrah. That ain't no boy." She chuckled again until a paroxym of coughing shook her emaciated body. "I'll cheat the hangman yet," she promised. "See if I don't!"

Angry now, Sir Francis bent down and pulled at the creature lying on the straw, but then recoiled with horror. The eyes which had flashed with spirit so often before him were now sunk into their sockets and her once dark and lustrous curls hung dull and filthy about her pale face.

"Robyn," he said hoarsely. "My God, what has brought you to this?"

She just stared at him as if she had never seen him before. He kneeled down at her side, drawing her into his arms. Her head fell back against his shoulder as if she had not the strength to hold it up. As his arms went around her he realised she had grown terribly thin. No one in Newgate ate properly unless they were willing to pay for the privilege and he suspected somehow that she would have had neither the means nor the inclination.

"Robyn," he said again. "Show me that you know I am here."

"Sir Francis," she said in a weak voice. "Oh, I prayed you would not find me here. Please go, I beg of you."

"Hush. The saints be praised it is not too late. They say you are convicted of highway robbery. How did it happen and why did you allow the lie to be accepted as the truth?"

"Because it is true."

Her voice faded away and he asked, "Why, Robyn? Why did you go? Were you forced?"

"I ran away, but no one made me. I had to go . . ."

A look of pain crossed his face. "But why did you admit to a crime you did not commit?"

"It was easier. I was there. No one would have believed me if I had said I was innocent. It was Captain Blackwell's idea, to get some money to take us to France, but it went horribly wrong.

Captain Blackwell escaped with my jewels, which I had given him for safe-keeping, and I was taken."

"You should have let me know, Robyn. I am sure I could have avoided this terrible ordeal."

"It will soon be over."

"No! You will soon be out of here."

"You do not understand. I want to die."

He drew back and then, taking off his coat he wrapped it around her. "You cannot know what you are saying. This place is enough to turn anyone's brain."

She laughed softly. "I do know what I am saying. It is better for you to leave me to die. And put your coat back on before it is taken from me."

He got to his feet once more. "I will make sure it is not. Robyn," he said, looking down at her as emotion welled up inside him, "forgive me for leaving you now, but I must make haste if I am to secure your release from this place with no further delay."

"Do not trouble, Sir Francis. You will soon be done with me for good. I am sorry I have been such a trial to you."

"I shall not delay by arguing with you, but take heart, I shall not rest until you are free again."

He hurried across the cell, pushing aside all those who importuned him for help. He called angrily for the turn-key who came scurrying towards him. Whilst he was obliged to wait to be let out a prisoner rushed up to him, waving a pair of breeches in the air.

"A guinea, your lordship. A guinea for them is all I ask!"

The gate swung open and feeling sick at heart, Sir Francis went out. As the key rasped in the lock again he peered across to where Robyn was huddled once again in the corner. His eyes filled with pain and his hand gripped the bars convulsively before he turned to the jailer.

To the fellow's astonishment he tossed a full purse of coins into his grimy hands.

"Now listen to me, my man, and listen well. Miss Wentworth, for that is her name, is to be transferred immediately to a cell of her own."

The turn-key weighed the purse in his hands, staring at it avariciously. "Ain't no rules against that, yer lordship. Had I known she was Quality . . ."

"She's to be given eatable food at regular intervals and water with which to wash. Is that clear to you?"

"Yes, yer lordship. Anything you say."

"To make certain it is done, my own servant will remain here until I am able to return. Miss Wentworth's maid will be arriving with clothing and personal belongings before long and I trust you will allow her in the cell."

"Can 'ardly refuse, can I, yer worship? Rely on Bert 'uggins. Treat 'er like a princess, I will."

The man quickly pocketed the coins and began to hurry after the unexpected benefactor. "A good long time since we had a Quality 'anging, yer worship."

Sir Francis paused then to eye the man coldly, resisting the temptation of assaulting him for his presumption.

In a voice low and husky with emotion he answered, "There will be no hanging, even if I have to go to the King himself!"

Thirteen

Sir Francis had suspected that no legal procedure could help his ward at this stage, and his lawyer confirmed the fact.

He had never dreamed the day would arrive when he might be obliged to seek payment for that old debt, for serving his King had been payment enough, but undoubtedly a royal pardon was the only way to save her now and he experienced no qualms about asking for one. Why Robyn had acted so rashly and why she wished to throw away her life, were questions that must remain unanswered until she was safe again, for that was the only matter which concerned him.

One thing he did not reckon upon was that the King had gone to Windsor. The delay which involved leaving Robyn in that hellhole for longer than was absolutely necessary, irked him as he left Mrs Fordingbridge and Lady Clyde to comfort each other, and set out once again—this time for Windsor.

On his arrival he was informed that the King was indisposed and could not see anyone. Frustration raged inside him, for at all times a mental picture was before him of the conditions in which the girl was confined, and he somehow felt, illogically, that perhaps he was in some way to blame.

"Pray tell His Majesty that it is Sir Francis Derringham who craves an audience, and that it is a matter of life and death."

The King's secretary knew of Sir Francis, as did most of those who were close to the monarch, and he agreed to convey the message. Even so, Sir Francis was obliged to spend an agonising two hours in an anteroom, alone with his own tortured thoughts.

When it seemed he could bear to wait no longer, a footman arrived to escort him to the King's chamber. The King did indeed look ill, Sir Francis observed, and he regretted the necessity of disturbing him.

"Sir Francis," King George greeted him as he bowed low. "It is many years since we met, but the circumstances of it are still clear in my mind. Sit down and tell me what brings you to Windsor so precipitately."

"Firstly, I must beg Your Majesty's pardon for the intrusion."

"Not at all. I have made it clear I am always available to you."

"Your Majesty, I am deeply sensible of the honour."

"I only hope I may be able to be of service to you at long last."

The King sat down on a sofa and then as His Majesty indicated he should do so, Sir Francis seated himself opposite to him.

"For some six months, sir, I have been guardian to the orphaned daughter of some old friends of mine, and in brief the girl has become involved with a blackguard."

The King looked pained. "Ah, how often I have heard that lament. It seems our children are born to pain us, Sir Francis. The Prince of Wales of late . . . Well, that is of no account. Pray continue."

"Your Majesty, as a result, Miss Wentworth is now in Newgate Jail, condemned of highway robbery, although I can assure Your Majesty that she is wholly innocent of any guilt and drawn into the sad business through no fault of her own."

The King appeared taken aback. "It is indeed a shocking tale, Sir Francis, and no doubt you are looking to me to issue a pardon for your ward."

"If Your Majesty pleases."

"Highway robbery is a serious crime and far too prevalent for my liking. However, I accept your assurances on her innocence and you must know I will grant you anything within my power."

Sir Francis felt as though a great weight had been lifted from his shoulders. As the King got to his feet he did so too.

"That will render me for ever in your debt, Your Majesty, and I am as ever your most faithful servant."

"You have already proved that beyond all doubt, Sir Francis. What I am about to do is a most trifling matter."

"Not to me, sir, and certainly not to my ward who is in danger of her life."

"Pray summon a servant, so my secretary may be called."

Sir Francis went to do so with alacrity and when he returned the King said, "The experience of a spell in one of my prisons cannot help but chasten her. Do you have plans for her future?"

Sir Francis hesitated for a moment or two and then answered, "If she will have me, sir, I intend to marry her."

The King laughed. "If! My good fellow, if she does not, she would be better placed in Bedlam!"

* * *

The sounds of Mrs. Fordingbridge's muffled wails met Sir Francis as he strode into his house, weary but triumphant. He intended to pause only long enough to have horses put to his carriage ready to collect Robyn from the jail, and after giving instructions for this to be done without delay he made haste to the small drawing room to impart the good news.

Waving the pardon, he looked around triumphantly. The scene was much as he had left it with Lady Clyde comforting the distraught Mrs Fordingbridge on the sofa.

"You may cease your wailing, ladies, for I have the King's pardon," he declared, but to his dismay the woman only cried harder into her handkerchief.

Lady Clyde looked at him, her eyes filling with tears and her lips trembling. "Oh, Francis . . ."

His smile faded but before he could question their attitude a footstep behind him caused Sir Francis to turn on his heel. He stiffened angrily, "Peters, did I not instruct you clearly enough to remain at Newgate with Miss Wentworth until I returned?"

"You did indeed, sir, and I endeavoured to obey. The maidservant is still with Miss Wentworth, only once the procession made off I deemed it time to seek you out. There was very little time to waste, sir."

The baronet's eyes narrowed. "Procession? What are you on about?"

"The procession to Tyburn, sir. Today is hanging day and Miss Wentworth's name was posted."

"*What*?" He gripped hold of the man. "When did it leave Newgate?"

The servant glanced at the clock on the mantel. "Almost two hours ago, sir."

"Two hours! My God, it must be there by now."

He let the man go and still clutching the pardon he flung out into the hall. "Pray God I am not too late!"

Robyn was scarcely aware of what was going on around her. The time she had spent in Newgate had passed as if it were part of a particularly nasty nightmare. The journey from the jail had proceeded at a snail's pace and seemed agonisingly slow. She only wished for the entire matter to be done with, but hanging days were also fete days for a large section of the population and they wished to make the most of them.

Ella had brought one of her new gowns to the jail and insisted that she wear it rather than the shirt and breeches in which she had fled from Albemarle Street, but now it was utterly ruined by the rotten fruit some onlookers had seen fit to throw. Most of those who followed the carts through the streets of London were not so cruel though. They pressed nosegays of flowers on those who made their last journey, and at every instance offered gin to deaden the pain of what was to come. Robyn wanted none of it. The pain of dying on the gallows could not be so great as that which she carried within her now. She could feel nothing more intensely than that and knew it was best she should die now the knowledge she carried within her grew too heavy to bear.

Inevitably she thought of Sir Francis although every nerve in her body strove to cast him from her mind. She wondered if he still sought a way of winning her freedom. As an honourable man she supposed he would do everything in his power to help her, and he would know true grief when his efforts failed. But not as much grief as he might have suffered if he knew the truth though. Far from wishing to injure him any more, all Robyn wanted to do was spare him, so the secret she had nursed for six long months would go with her to the grave. Any sorrow he might experience and the disgrace would soon fade, and the pleasurable life of the *beau monde* was bound to heal his wounded sensibilities before too long a time passed.

The procession finally reached its destination and the crowd was so great even she was surprised at the number of people who would want to see an execution. Today they would be delighted, for three felons were to be hanged at once, and one of them being a lady of breeding, beautiful too, excited the crowd to a frenzy.

Three nooses were already hanging from the gallows and despite her detached feelings Robyn was obliged to avert her face as the constables struggled to cleave a path for the carts.

Realising there was now but little time left, Robyn stooped to speak to Ella who had faithfully remained with her mistress. "Ella, listen to me."

The woman looked at her, raising a damp handkerchief to her tear-stained cheeks. "Oh, ma'am, I cannot credit this is happening. Sir Francis must come soon."

A quiver of pain shot through Robyn's body at the mention of his name and then once again she thrust all thoughts of him aside. "Ella, I must be quick now. There is little time left. Tell Mrs. Fordingbridge I am sorry for the grief I have caused her, thank Lady Clyde for all her kindness, and finally I wish you to have all my clothes which remain at Albemarle Street. Is that clear?"

The girl answered with a muffled sob before she asked in a choked voice, "Is there anything you would have me say to Sir Francis?"

Robyn stared ahead, down the length of Park Lane which was bathed in spring sunshine, the scene of so many happy occasions if only she had appreciated that fact at the time.

"Only tell him I am myself responsible for my downfall. No one else is to be held to blame."

Ella began to sob anew as the carts were positioned beneath the gallows. The spectacle was enjoyed so much more when all the executions took place at one time.

Bracing herself for the inevitable now she was surprised when one of the other condemned prisoners began a drunken tirade, blaming his downfall on everything, including the law. Despite his condition he was quite obviously terrified, a circumstance recognised by the crowd, who began to pelt him with rotten fruit and other revolting objects.

"Let the wench speak now!" came a cry.

"Let us hear the doxy's story."

The young man in the next cart who had been cowering in one corner of it, nudged her as best he could, being manacled and wearing a halter about his neck.

"It's you they want. Go on, speak to them. Why do you hesitate?"

"What . . . do I speak about?" she asked, somewhat taken aback.

"They want to know what brought you to ruin."

"Oh no! I could not. I cannot speak of it."

"For God's sake! Do you not understand? The more of us who speak to the crowd, the longer it'll be before . . ."

The crowd were shouting for her to speak, but she shook her head.

"If yer want to say yer piece, get on with it," the hangman said. "I'm not paid to wait here all day."

She looked at him fearfully as he leaned over her and she could not help but shudder at the sight of his ugly hands and leering mouth. "Can't wait to turn *you* off, my lovely."

"Go on!" the young man urged again, "Or are you waiting to be launched into eternity."

She stepped forward to face the rabble, blinking back the tears she feared she might, after all, shed. The smell was even more nauseating than in Newgate although she had grown used to it there. There would be no time for her to grow accustomed to this.

"Speak. Come on, let's hear your tale. I'll warrant it's a good one!"

The crowd cheered and Robyn swallowed the lump in her throat. She had never faced such a crowd before. They were an ugly assortment, made good-natured by the prospect of a spectacle.

"The story of my downfall began before I was even born . . ." she began.

"Speak up. Let us hear!"

"I had never known the love of a father," she went on, projecting her voice as best she could.

The crowd groaned and her head drooped, but when she realised that the hangman was testing his knots she looked up again.

" 'Tis a tragic tale that led me to ruin," she said to calls from the audience, "but I do not seek to be absolved from blame for the crime of which I stand here convicted."

Her voice began to fade somewhat and the young man beside her started to dance about in distress. "Why don't you get on with it?"

She took a deep breath. "Up until six months ago I was but a simple country girl. Then, on his death bed, the man I had always looked upon as my father related to me a tale which so shocked me I believe it unhinged my reason for a time."

Robyn hesitated, realising almost everyone within hearing was listening with great interest and she decided at that moment that she actually wanted to share her burden before she died.

"A sad tale he told me with his last breath. My mother, so beautiful and beloved, was seduced by a heartless rake who once he had had his way moved on to new diversions, leaving her to bear both her own shame and his child. My mother died of that shame soon after I was born and her husband spent the rest of his life reflecting on bitterness with no time for the child who bore his name, a constant reminder and mockery. However, I soon discovered that worse was to come. As he came to the end of his tale he revealed that he had taken steps to revenge himself on the rake who had caused his torment and he informed me that he had conferred me to the guardianship of the very man who had ruined my mother."

The crowd, who were accustomed to the drunken grovelling of those about to hang, had rarely been entertained so well, and in a choked voice Robyn went on, "Living beneath his roof was well nigh unbearable day after day, so great was my hatred of this man, but it was a feeling I could not maintain however hard I tried, and I finally fell under the spell of his charm, just as my mother had done. Against my will I came to love this man, which you may consider only natural, but it was not the love of a daughter for her father. It was the love of a woman for a man."

There was a short pause before she continued, "That is what drove me from his house into the clutches of an evil man, and that is also the reason I cannot regret I am to die. The caress of the hangman's noose will be welcome to free me from this torment I can no longer bear."

For a moment there was a stunned silence from the crowd and then realising she had confessed to hundreds of delighted onlookers a fact that she had scarcely dared admit to herself, Robyn slumped back into the cart, tears streaming down her cheeks whilst a great cheer arose from the crowd.

They were all certain no future hanging day could ever be so good as this.

Fourteen

Sir Francis rode as far as possible and when he
could go no further on horseback he proceeded
on foot with an army of his servants pushing a
way clear for him. Some of the people crowding
forward resented his presumption, but most
recognised he was Quality and did not demur.
Progress, however, was far from quick and in
his fever to reach the gallows he angrily pushed
away the pedlars and beggars who would insist
on importuning him.

At last he moved near and with great relief
realised the executions had not yet taken place.
He silently thanked Providence for the custom
of the condemned addressing the crowd. However, as he drew nearer his eyes opened wide
with surprise to see it was Robyn herself standing upon the scaffold saying her piece.

His heart ached to see her there, among the common criminals, the scum of the land, but he had the means to win her freedom which spurred him on.

Despite his anxiety to free her as soon as possible from her ordeal he did notice that she was holding the crowd spellbound, an unusual occurrence at a hanging. He paused then to listen as her voice grew stronger but his eyes narrowed as the gist of what she was saying reached his ears at last and then he plunged closer to the scaffold.

When she reached the end of her sad tale he stood pale-faced at the base of the gallows, stunned and disbelieving.

"Hell's teeth!" he cried, but in the midst of the noise all around no one heard him.

He stared hard at the distraught and unknowing figure only a few yards away before he became aware of Ella, weeping bitterly nearby. Although he was a man shaken to the core by what Robyn had revealed, he collected himself and reached out for the city marshal, shouting to be heard above the din, "I am Sir Francis Derringham and I have come direct from the King with a pardon for this prisoner."

The man read the document with agonising slowness before he climbed up onto the scaffold, saying, "It's a pardon. A King's pardon for the wench!"

A great cheer went up amongst the crowd, although there were some who jeered at being robbed of their sport.

Robyn looked dazedly around her, aware of a great furore but of nothing else. Suddenly Sir Francis climbed up on the scaffold too and she cowered away, believing him to be only a figment of her imagination.

"Robyn," he said gently, aware of her shocked and uncomprehending condition, "I have come to take you home."

Her lips moved as if she wanted to speak and when she stepped forward, her legs grew weak and she pitched forward into his arms instead in a dead faint.

As the long-case clock on the landing chimed the hour, Sir Francis, as he walked slowly up the stairs, took out his timepiece and glanced at it. When he reached Robyn's apartment he hesitated outside for a moment or two before knocking lightly on the door. When he went in it was to find Mrs Fordingbridge getting to her feet. She had been embroidering a cap which she put down quickly, giving him a smile of welcome.

"Sir Francis, how nice to see you."

"I trust I do not call at an inopportune moment," he said with uncharacteristic diffidence.

"Not at all. Indeed, I was hoping that you

would. I really need to have words with Mrs Maggs, so perchance you could bear Robyn company for a few minutes whilst I am gone."

"An honour, ma'am."

He held the door open for her and when she had gone he turned at last to regard Robyn herself. She was sitting upright in the centre of a chaise longue, her hands demurely folded in her lap. For once her hair was tied back in a simple style and she was wearing a brown woollen gown so drab he was certain it must have travelled with her from Devonshire. Her cheeks still bore an unnatural pallor despite Ella's efforts with the haresfoot and rouge, and as she raised her eyes to his there remained deep shadows beneath them.

"How do you feel today?" he asked hesitantly.

"Well, I thank you, Sir Francis," she answered in a dull voice.

"The fever has thankfully gone, but you should not yet be out of your bed."

"I assure you I am quite recovered."

He smiled faintly. "We feared it was gaol fever which afflicted you. It was a great relief to learn that it was not."

He came across the room and, standing before her, he placed his hand beneath her chin, turning her face first this way and that so he could scrutinise it carefully whilst her eyes remained downcast.

"A spell of rustication would be beneficial, I think. The good country air will soon put the colour back into your cheeks and a sparkle in your eyes."

When she made no answer he stepped back and she averted her face. Then she said, "I only wonder you do not wish to send me to a nunnery."

"Oh, I do not think that would be at all the thing." Continuing to gaze at her profile he added, "It isn't true, you know, Robyn."

She turned to look at him then, her eyes filling with pain. "So you intend to deny it. I am not surprised, neither do I blame you."

"Your mother was a very beautiful woman. For a while when I was no older than you are now, I was amongst many other men who loved her. I did my utmost, in my foolish way, to make her love me and I think she was amused by my pranks, but, Robyn, she and I were never lovers."

She stared at him for a few moments as if she could not quite credit what he had said. Then she turned away again, pleating and unpleating her skirt in her agitation.

"Why did you not speak of it to me at the very beginning?" she asked. "We could have avoided so much grief."

She pressed her trembling fingers to her lips. "I could not. If you knew and would not acknowledge it, or if you did not know it was all the same. I could not speak of it to you, for I was so eaten up with hatred and anger, and then, later . . .”

He took her hand and cradled it in his. "Whose by-blow can I be?” she asked in a whisper.

"During these past few days I have thought back to that time in as much detail as I can remember. Your mother had the reputation of being a virtuous woman and your father—Colonel Wentworth—who was older, appeared unfashionably jealous. I am convinced that he really is your father, but an insane jealousy of my attachment to his wife caused him to attribute the blame to me. Perhaps she was even vain enough to boast of it initially, before she became aware of the dire effect upon Colonel Wentworth.”

Again she turned slowly to look at him. "Do you truly believe that?”

"Yes,” he answered simply. "I am certain that is the true answer to this sad business.”

She shook her head. " ’Tis very much like *Othello*, is it not?”

"Not really. Your father did not murder Mrs Wentworth.”

She gave him a mournful look. "He did—with neglect, with jealousy, removing her from the social life she loved. The effect was the same. She died of grief.” She drew a deep sigh. "Such suffering for no reason.”

"It is over now."

The smile which flickered across her face was the first one he had seen for a long time. "Next time any one declares God Save the King, I shall recall that the King saved me, or rather," she added breathlessly, "it was your supreme effort."

"You must think no more about it. I shall not. You cannot have thought I would have let it happen."

She shook her head again. "I cannot now conceive what I did think." She stiffened and drew away from him slightly. "Have you news of Captain Blackwell?"

His face took on a look of hardness as he flicked a speck of dust from his otherwise immaculate breeches. "He has fled to France and will not return, for he must know that if he does I will kill him," he answered in an unemotional voice.

"He is a wicked man, I cannot deny, but I encouraged him to take me away. He cannot be held entirely to blame."

"That is of no account any more so do not distress yourself further. Of the only importance now is the fact that you are safe."

"Oh, I have made a complete cake of myself for so long. Even my jewels, such as they were, are gone now."

"I possess one of the finest collections of

jewellery in England, and if nothing in it pleases you you can select some elsewhere."

She gasped, looking at him with a mixture of surprise and wonder as he raised her hand to his lips. "There cannot be many men who receive a declaration of love in the shadow of the Tyburn Tree. Mine," he went on, looking at her now, "must be made in more mundane surroundings."

"How can you?" she asked in wonderment. "I have behaved like a virago towards you since the day I arrived."

"I trust that is all in the past," he answered dryly.

She continued to gaze at him adoringly for a few moments before leaning over to kiss his cheek rather diffidently, but before she had a chance he had taken her in his arms and was kissing her lips.

When he drew away, leaving her breathless, he said, "Dare I hope to persuade you to give up your dream of spinsterhood."

Putting her head on his shoulder she sighed. "That was made only because I feared being trapped in the kind of misery in which my parents found themselves." She looked at him again. "So short a time ago there seemed to be nothing worth living for."

The memory caused her eyes to cloud again and in an effort to blot it out he kissed her again. She clung to him, allowing herself to respond at last, now that all the shadows had passed.

At length, Mrs Fordingbridge returned whereupon she became immediately flustered and made excuses to withdraw again. Neither Robyn nor Sir Francis made any attempt to stop her before becoming lost in one another again.

Let COVENTRY Give You
A Little Old-Fashioned Romance

8057